Choose Life

A Novel By

Brian Nelson

DEDICATION

To the one and only true and living God! I'm glad that you don't have to ask for man's permission, nor do you seek the opinions of man to perform your work through someone. Thank you!

Table of Contents

COLLISION COURSE: Today's Choices Set in Motion Tomorrow's paths 1
Short-term Choices Long-term Consequences 7
When adversity chooses you 16
Choosing the Right Company/Friends 20
The Chosen One 26
The Meeting: Choose a side 30
Choosing to Continue down the Wrong Path 33
The High Cost of Choosing to Do Nothing 38
Family Choices 43
Face to Face with Choice 48
The same bad choice again, and again, and again! 53
Bad choices, Bad consequences 58
The Right Choice over the Popular Choice 62
Choices, remembering who you are 66
Confronted by a Choice 69
Choices that Reveal the Condition of the Heart 75
We get to Choose the path that we travel in life 81
Choices affect those closest to you 87
Wrong Choices come with Unintended Consequences 91
The right Choice over the easy Choice 95
Time sensitive choices 98
Decisions during times of Crisis 101
"The Ultimate choice" 106
Choices come with Short-term and Long-term consequences 111
Choices with harsh realities attached 113
When the choice of hate is stronger than love 118
Blinded by our choices 121
Choose Life defined 126
Choose Life lived 132

CHAPTER 1

COLLISION COURSE: Today's Choices Set in Motion Tomorrow's paths

It was a cool Fall morning in the city of Chicago and an up and coming business executive, Conrad James, was up at the crack of dawn deep in thought. He was at peace as he watched the leaves fall in his back yard while sipping on a predawn cup of coffee. Conrad had come to a major decision in his life. Presented with a choice that would have ramifications far beyond what was currently occupying his mind.

As a first-generation college graduate from his family and one of the few African American men on the prestigious campus of the University of Chicago, Conrad was a man on the rise in the field of Engineering.

He was molded into the man he is today in large part because of the choices made by his mother years ago. As a single mom growing up in the Henry Horner Projects on the west side of Chicago, she decided that she wanted something different for her soon to be born son. She was determined to start breaking the mold of young black men growing up in America's inner-city environments starting with what was to some a simple act, but to her one of great significance. She would launch him into life with a unique and different name she hoped would distinguish him from all the other boys growing up there.

So, she named him Conrad to send a message to him and to those who he encounters. "This young black male is not to be placed in a category or put into any box." She would always say.

Conrad excelled in school in all his class subjects but was

especially gifted in mathematics. Math became a second language to Conrad and he could visualize it without the need to write things down. Possessing a genius in mathematics that no one around him could even begin to comprehend. People simply said he was "gifted by God" in the field of mathematics.

Conrad received a full scholarship to the University of Chicago and not only graduated at the top of his class, but he acquired advanced degrees in the field of Quantum Engineering as well.

Conrad was 6'4" with an athletic build and he excelled in sports. The norm for a kid growing up with his height and athleticism from his neighborhood was to become committed to sports and use it as a way out. However, Conrad was always different and taught by his mother to work to defeat narrow stereotypes and self-imposed limits.

"Not bad for a kid from Henry Horner projects" he said out loud, but to no one, encouraging himself as he was taking everything in on this cool Sunday morning before heading to church.

He made the right choices most of his life and was at peace with his current decision. He was ready to inform his wife Janice and his only son Jordan of the decision he made once they were awake. To Conrad this was a moment of reflection, thankfulness and hopeful excitement about the immediate future.

"Good morning baby!" Conrad joyfully said to his beautiful wife Janice as she broke through the silence of the moment Conrad was having to himself.

"Good morning darling" - said Janice "you look to be in deep thought this morning is everything ok?"

Everything is great! Conrad said perking up with excitement. In fact, I have some news. I've decided to accept the position as the new CEO of Houston Exponential Engineering (HEE) in Houston,

TX. The one we have been talking and praying about and I wanted to make sure you were the first person to know it before I notified them. I also want to thank you for all your help in getting me to this moment. Conrad said.

I already knew that said Janice with a playful wave of the hand. It's not news to me even if it is to you. In fact, I have already been planning the move and getting things in order Janice continued. They both laughed hysterically!!

You want to know why my mom named me Conrad? He asked reflectively while looking in the distance at the Chicago skyline from their condo on Lake Shore Drive. Conrad's mood reverted back to serene. She always wanted me to be different, to stand out.

"She'd always say no one will expect to see a black man named Conrad, so they'll never be ready for what you represent" Conrad recalled nostalgically thinking about his mother who died 10 years ago. The only thing more different than a black man named Conrad is a black man who studies Quantum Engineering, he laughed. I wish she could see me today Conrad said. Your mother was a woman of vision! She already saw you today even before you became the man you are now responded Janice grabbing his hand and wiping a tear from his face.

They would be packing up and making their way to the city of Houston, TX along with their 18-year-old son Jordan within the next two months. Conrad and Janice were at a point in their life and marriage where they were as happy as ever before. It felt like they were at an apex in their lives looking down from the top of a mountain. They could not have known these current choices before them today were leading them into one of the greatest challenges of their lives. Choices that would test their love for one another, for others and their faith that has gotten them to this point.

Harry Jacobs grew up in a small town in south Texas. Like a lot of boys from the great state of Texas, he always wanted to play college football for the University of Texas Longhorns, only Harry was never quite good enough an athlete to reach the top level of college sports. Harry in fact, was cut from his varsity high school football team during school tryouts three years in a row. For Harry, each time he was cut from the team seemed more devastating than the last. Never quite big enough, strong enough, or fast enough to compete at a high level, Harry felt like even God himself had shortchanged him of the gifts he needed to fulfill his dreams.

It appeared to Harry he was always being told no, to wait, being rejected and overlooked or worst - not being noticed at all.

With each perceived rejection, the weight of his burden appeared to get heavier and heavier. Harry loved football and made himself into a pretty good football player through his great work ethic and the passion he possessed for the game. However, his athletic ability simply never matched his passion for the game burning inside of him.

He was even told by his dad that the way he would become noticed and make it to the top would be through academics not football. Not quite what a 17-year old boy with football dreams on his mind wanted to hear, but he did realize he was good in school and loved math.

Harry still wanted to attend the University of Texas but at 5ft 10in and only 165lbs he accepted the reality given to him by his dad.

Harry's dad approached him on a hot and humid Texas day while he was in the back of the house practicing moves he saw the players using at practice from his high school team. Junior, we need to talk his dad Harry Sr. said to him.

Sure, Dad what's up?

"Son, I've been watching you practice for a while now and its time you face the facts. You are just not good enough!" Harry Sr. said bluntly. Hurt, stunned, and taken aback by the bluntness and lack of compassion from his dad, Harry Jr. sat there in stunned silence. Harry felt the sting of rejection once again from his dad. It seemed at least to Harry that his dad was disappointed in him for not being able to carry on the family tradition of excelling in sports. His dad was a standout running back at Texas, and his grandfather as well, but not Harry.

This was not the first-time Harry Jr felt the sting of rejection from his dad. Although Harry Sr. was not a cruel man by nature, he was one who found it
difficult to show affection to his son or anyone else. He is what one would consider a hard man, a Texas cowboy who could fight with the best of them.

Another hurtful time for Harry Jr. happened one night as he overheard his dad on the telephone with someone who asked about his son playing football. Harry Sr. started mocking the lack of athletic ability of his son to the person on the phone. A devastating conversation deeply hurtful for the struggling teenager at the time. And now, here was his hero telling him to his face to give up on his dream of college sports because he was simply "not good enough". Those words echoed in his head for years and followed him into adulthood.

This may not have been the first-time Harry was hurt and made to feel like he didn't measure up at home, but Harry vowed it would be his last.

"I'm going to win a full academic scholarship to the University of Texas" Harry said. "And then I'm going to become the CEO of a major engineering company right here in the heart of Texas" Harry promised himself with tears streaming uncontrollably down his face. "Once I'm off to college, I'm never going to return to this house, at least not until I'm CEO of a major company, maybe then my dad will be proud of me.

My dad will probably never even notice that I'm gone anyway, he never has before!" Said Harry.

Fueled by his rejection Harry did achieve a full academic scholarship to the University of Texas.

    Two men -Conrad James and Harry Jacobs with seemingly nothing in common, one from a small town in South Texas the other from the Westside of Chicago. On the surface, it would appear to be highly unlikely they would have a direct impact on each other's lives or even meet, but through the choices set before them, the ebb and flow of life and the providence of God, they were set on a path destined to link them together forever. They could not have known at the time but the two of them had embarked on a collision course. They would soon become as much a part of each other's life story as any other person they had ever met.

CHAPTER 2

Short-term Choices Long-term Consequences

Andre Jackson rose to the position of News Editor with the number one local news station in Houston WKROC.

He was now in the number two position for the station and was the highest ranking African American in the local news market in the city of Houston. The only person who was ahead of him was his old mentor and friend Paul Wilson.

Paul, a Caucasian male from the "good side" of Houston took a liking to the younger Andre, a black man from Houston's rough Fifth ward, known as one of the city's poorest ghettos.

When Andre came to the station right out of college ten years ago, he and Paul immediately formed an unlikely bond that benefitted them both, helping them rise to positions of power in the local news market in the city of Houston, TX.

Paul loved country music, going to rodeos and to the Museum of Fine Arts, Houston from time to time. Andre's choice of music like most from his Fifth Ward neighborhood centered around the legendary Gangster Rap group the Ghetto Boys and their record label Rap-A-Lot records who together became pioneers for southern rap music.

Paul taught the brilliant young Andre everything he would need to know about the business and even some things he probably didn't need. He learned all the technical aspects of the business, also the people side. But more than anything, he taught Andre how to excel in the ratings game of news cycles and to understand without ratings neither of them would survive.

They would meet frequently after work for drinks and talk about the day's activities. However, they also had regularly scheduled Tuesday evening meetings which were more formal in nature. It was in these Tuesday meetings that Paul would do most of his teaching with Andre as he saw great potential in the up and coming young executive. Paul could see the intense desire Andre possessed, a passion for the news media industry as well as career success.

Andre and his wife Daphne were happily married for eight years and were gifted with a beautiful daughter named Renae six years ago. Predictably, all the evening meetings were beginning to be a problem for Andre at home causing friction with his wife and daughter so Andre decided he would address it with Paul at their next Tuesday meeting. He witnessed what the choice of choosing career over family did to Paul's marriages as he was now three years divorced from his third wife.

Prior to Andre being offered the position of News Director with WKROC in Houston, Paul Wilson reached out to him, informing Andre via email he was contemplating some important issues he wanted to address with him at this Tuesday's meeting. Andre was curious and attempted to press Paul for information, but he declined. This is something we need to discuss face to face Andre said Paul.

Paul was a little nervous about having this conversation but deemed it necessary to see where Andre stood on the issue prior to offering him the position of News Director even though he greatly hoped Andre would be agreeable.

On a hot July night where in Houston nighttime temperatures can be near 90 degrees, they met in the corner of one of their local taverns to have the conversation.

Hey what's going on Paul? Said Andre with anticipation ringing in his voice.

Thanks for coming Paul responded quickly, ready to get down to business.

Andre, I believe you and I make a great team he continued. As you know I have been promoted to the position of General Manager of the station which means I will be the one hiring my replacement as News Director. My hope is it's you who would be the one to fill it. I know you have what it takes talent wise, but what I need to know is just how badly you want the position and how far you are willing to go in the direction I have envisioned. Paul delivered.

I want it badly Paul! Andre said, but I'm not sure exactly what you mean by how far I'm willing to go.

Andre, there are some harsh realities of this business that I don't always agree with, but remember I've always told you that ratings, ratings, ratings were the name of the game.

Of course, I remember, you say it all the time. How can I ever forget? Andre laughed nervously

Good! said Paul because the goal here is to keep WKROC the number one station in Houston with us at the top. After that, who knows where we can end up. Andre was never one to mince words; get to the harsh realities! He interrupted. Andre was growing impatient but excited.

Ratings are a function of sensationalism and the more sensational the better the ratings Paul continued. So, what I'll be expecting in my next News Director Andre is this, "we must continue to push minority stereotypes, continue to bombard the public with black and brown faces whenever there is a crime committed -

especially if it's a high-profile crime and then highlight their apprehension and capture."

What? Said Andre in amazement.

Yes, said Paul, and I hope you don't take any of this personal Andre, this is why I wanted to discuss it with you directly, and face to face.

I never realized you held these racist views Paul I'm shocked!

It's not a question of race Andre, said Paul casually. The hell it's not! Andre interjected, pounding his fist on the table in anger and generating quick glances from the other patrons at the tavern.

I brought you here for this meeting to show you the bigger picture of how the media market game works. Said Paul.

I don't give a damn about your "bigger picture" Andre yelled. What you mean is another way to continue the same old bullshit in America that has always gone on. The people at the top getting bigger, maintaining their power, while the people at the bottom get smaller and have no power. How we've been able to sell this crap to the masses all these years is amazing to me said Andre.

Most people want security Andre not power. Paul said sharply.

Both men started to get louder and their responses more forceful with each back and forth response. This went on for about two minutes as tensions in the air started rising as hot as the Houston mid-summer night heat. It appeared to others they were about to come to blows.

A slender built waitress came to the table "is everything alright? Can I get you boys anything?" She asked hoping to

calm the gentlemen and to ensure a tip. No, we're fine mam but thanks for asking said Paul maintaining his constant southern charm. This gave Paul an opportunity to calm his voice and try to take control of the conversation. I want you to look and think long-term Andre. I have connected with you since you first came to WKROC right out of college because I could see in you a talent and drive for
this industry that stood out above the rest.

Now calm down for a moment before these people call the police on us, so I can paint the picture a little clearer for you. Paul continued.

First off you know I'm no racist otherwise we would not have the relationship that we have developed over these last 10 years. I'm also now friends with your wife Daphne. But to keep this station number one in this politically charged environment with all the anti-immigration rhetoric, and divisions in America we have a prime opportunity to do great things for our careers and our families by making the station number one.

"We need to constantly bombard the public with negative images of black and brown people to compete in this market for media ratings. It's the primary method used to get ahead in today's media market" Paul stated unemotionally. It's nothing personal, it's the ratings game and everyone's playing it, we must do the same if we want to survive in this industry.

Pointing out racial minorities and their characteristics while highlighting stereotypes creates panic and hysteria among the masses and this generates huge media viewership.

You mean white people when you say the masses? Andre interjected.

Yes. Said Paul. I don't know if you've noticed Andre, but people like to watch news channels they either agree with or confirm their personal biases and will give them comfort in knowing the "good guys" will protect them. I've noticed Paul. Fuck their comfort! Andre said.

So, when it's a white suspect or criminal exactly what would you have us to do then? Simply dismiss it and not report on it? Andre asked with sarcasm.

Of course, you want to report on it. Replied Paul. We'll simply be giving out more general and vague descriptions for whites instead of specifics like we'll do with the minority suspects. In fact, we won't even mention their race.

We'll have the news anchor say things like he's a 6ft 1in. male, of medium complexion, with black hair. And instead of repeatedly running the video for our viewers like we'll be doing with the minorities we'll run it once at the end of the news for white suspects when people have stopped listening anyway.

We'll also play the "mental illness card" on the white suspects when there are things like mass shootings. We know we must cover high profile incidents or be accused of neglect.

That's the new built in excuse for white men and those in power Andre mental illness, no one wants to believe the people in power are murders. These things can be handled Andre it's been an unwritten standard, an industry practice for years said Paul casually. It's like "alternative facts", that was classic.

Look Andre, I understand what I'm asking of you is an emotional issue and I know it's hard but so is the news business and you've got a choice to make. I need to know that I can count on you so we can take this station to heights it has never seen. And I promise you your career will also soar to heights which you never dreamed.

Paul, you are asking me to be a part of discrimination against my own people and thousands of others if not millions stated Andre. Not only is it wrong, I need to remind you that racial discrimination and any other kind of discrimination is also illegal in the "United States of America" Andre said with disgust in his voice.

Paul jumped back in "I know it's racism, but it's institutional racism so it is almost impossible to prove. Institutional racism is not personal Andre and it doesn't target individuals or call them by name." Said Paul.

The hell it's not! Andre replied. It blankets people with unnecessary burdens and hardships keeping them down and without hope. It's systematic, so it does irreparable damage to the lives of large numbers of people, and for much longer time periods. It's an invisible enemy, one easy to deny by those at the top and almost impossible to fight against by those at the bottom. It hurts blacks, whites and people of all races.

They both simply sat there for a moment being quiet and soaking in the thoughts of one another. The level of acrimony was now very thick in the air and they needed this time to compose themselves and gather their thoughts. Neither one quite sure what the other was thinking or knowing how to proceed.

After a few seconds, which seemed like hours, Paul finally spoke again. "Look Andre, I'm sorry I had to expose you to these hard truths about our industry and the way things are done. However, I believe in your talent and abilities, so I just wanted to make sure we got on the same page with this.

America wants what it wants and right now, Americans want to believe certain segments of society are safe. Those at the top are there to help them not hurt them. This frees them up to do what's best for everyone".

You really believe that? Andre asked incredulously.

"Don't you understand the news is now more entertainment and special interest driven than factual? We create the facts for people and we shape their realities. In this time when immigration is front and center (whether it's illegal or legal immigration), Americans are concerned about the repercussions of the issue.

We have to be able to provide them with a certain comfort level for the good of everyone" Paul said. The atmosphere was now back to calm. Both men had regained their composure and were collecting their thoughts.

Paul ended with justification for his philosophy. This is the game we must play, and I hope that you are with me on this. How badly do you want the things you say you want Andre? You do have a choice, but know that this will open a lot of opportunities for you and you can one day be in my position.

Maybe then you can change things in our industry, but you must change things from the inside, you have to have a seat at the table to eat. It's going to take both power and influence to change this industry but you need to make the right choice Paul said.

Stick with me Andre and you can be the next Ed Bradley. So, I'll ask you again how badly do you want to get ahead in this industry?

With calm restored, and Andre having trust in Paul, the two men shook hands and left with the understanding that Andre would accept the position of News Director reporting only to

Paul as his General Manager.

Even though Andre didn't agree morally with the things Paul was asking him to do, he told himself he was looking at the "big picture" as Paul called it. Hoping one day, despite his choice today to put aside his integrity for the moment, he would be in a position of change in the future not just for himself, but others as well. The reality was it was Paul's imputing of his longtime journalism hero Ed Bradly of 60 minutes fame, and his
personal quest for fame that influenced him the most and Andre would soon find out that choices have both long-term and life altering consequences.

Chapter 3
When adversity chooses you

Sun Park High School is one of the biggest and best high schools in the southeastern Texas region. Known for its beautiful college like campus, perfectly manicured lawns, and modern buildings. It's a high school representing the classic picture of suburban America. Possessing one of the top football teams in the country, it is also the home of a great modern technological center donated by one of its rich alumni. The Howard Fletcher Center which prominently displays his name.

The school has produced both great athletes and academics due to the abundance of financial resources its community has at its disposal. It sits in one of the most affluent communities in America.

However, amid the opulence and extravagance of the campus are two best friends. They have known one another since the first grade and live two houses away from one another. Oliver Jones and Henry Allen appear to be living a life in contradiction to the hope and excitement of the large high school campus. The two teenagers both 17-year-old juniors are finding it harder and harder to get up and ready to go to school each morning for they are the victims of merciless and relentless bullying on this "beautiful" campus and it appeared, at least to Oliver and Henry there is no way out.

The persecuting started back on the first day of the 2017 school year - their freshman year. And now as juniors on a mid-June hot and steamy day in Texas, the same two boys were walking to their first period classes when they are abruptly pushed down from behind by a group of three other boys who thought it would be a fun way to start off the school year with a good laugh at the expense of anyone who they perceived as "nerds".

The group was part of an online "anti-nerd club" started by local notorious school bully Owen Fletcher. Owen was constantly seeking attention and could care less about at who's expense his harassment was aimed.

Owen was the only son of Howard Fletcher, A great businessman and well known in the community of Sun Park, TX and the school's biggest donor and the person mostly responsible for the new and expansive state of the art technology center on the high school campus.

Howard Fletcher's wife divorced him a few years before because he would always choose his business ventures over her and their family. Unwilling to change his behavior, he's now making the same decisions with his son Owen, who is desperately in need of attention and affection from his father but has yet to receive it.

The online bullying club started playfully taking donations online not expecting to get much response, but just for fun, and meant as a joke. However, to their delightful surprise they started receiving donations from other kids at their school and eventually from students outside of the Sun Park High School community as well.

The donations amount was now up to over six hundred dollars with a new goal of one thousand dollars; this for whoever could make members of the group laugh the hardest at a disgraced boy or girl they considered to be a nerd during the first week of the new school year.

Later in the evening after surviving the first day of the new school year Oliver Jones called his childhood friend Henry Allen to see how he was doing.

Hi Henry, how's it going, you feeling better now with the first day of school out of the way? Oliver asked hopefully. Relieved is more like it, said Henry as he forced a smile to come over his face. I don't know if I can handle another school year like the last two years we've gone through Oliver.

It seems like the terrorizing is starting to get even more extreme Henry continued. Yeah, I know. Said Oliver in a sad tone. Do you think that we should go to the school administration again to see if we can get them to stop what's going on? Said Henry

Oliver started thinking out loud as he searched inwardly for a solution as to why he and his best friend Henry somehow became "special targets" of this relentless oppression at their school. He rehearsed in his mind some of the harsh treatment he and his friend have suffered there the last couple of years, and then quickly went on to list just a few of them with Henry.

We went to the school administration when our heads were dunked in the toilets as freshmen, we went to the school administration when some of them smashed cake in our faces during lunch hour, and we went to the school when we were put inside of our own lockers and humiliated during the school dance Oliver said to Henry in a dejected tone. These were only a few of the times they were made to feel ashamed, desperate, and hopeless at school and no one in the administration seemed concerned enough to put a stop to it.

The school looked like a crown jewel to Oliver's mom when she and her son moved into the community of Sun Park, TX a few years ago. His mom became hopeful of the future after overcoming the death of her husband. He made the grave mistake of choosing to drive after a night of drinking and never made it home.

His phone revealed that he sent a text message seconds before crashing. But this community and her new marketing job gave his mom hope and he was reluctant to take that from her like Drunk Driving took his dad.

It's been two full years of this hounding already and I don't think I can take another year like last year Henry repeated.

I know man Oliver replied feeling the helplessness that his friend expressed. Are you going to let your mom know again Oliver? said Henry, maybe she can set up another meeting between us and the school principal to finally get this to end. No Henry replied Oliver, my mom has enough on her plate with the new job, bills and all.

And besides, she finally seems to be smiling again after the death of my dad. I wish he was still here with us I bet things would be different said Oliver in a dejected tone. Tomorrow I think we should go into the principal's Office ourselves to see if he'll do anything to stop it.

Just as in previous times the Fletcher name limited the amount of discipline the school would administer to Owen Fletcher and his group of friends.   The two boy's biggest fears were now being realized. After they met with school administrators, the browbeating not only kept going but intensified and this event marked the beginning of a new phase of terrorizing the kids would have to endure. A type of intimidation that can be even more debilitating, cruel, ruthless, and sinister. Its progressively more intense, constant, and almost impossible to get away from. Cyber bullying!!!

CHAPTER 4

Choosing the Right Company/Friends

It was now twenty years since Harry Jacobs left the comfort of his father's home heading for the University of Texas at Austin. He became an honors student while majoring in Engineering. This fast tracked him to the position of Senior VP with Houston Exponential Engineering (HEE). Although only with the company for five years, Harry chose to use his disappointments in life as fuel to propel him in his career to a level he dared to dream of despite his perceived rejection from his father.

He showed his father, although he would not become the high-profile football player, that he could still make a name for himself. "I'm going to become the CEO of a major engineering company right here in the heart of Texas" Harry vowed to himself that day twenty years ago and now he was only one step away from achieving his goal.

This would be his redemption from the perceived disapproval of his father, and from University of Texas football. Harry always carried what he believed his father thought of him around like a weight, an unnecessary burden buried deep inside of him.

The resulting "root of bitterness" which occupied his heart was allowed to grow unrestrained manifesting in a harsh temper capable of overwhelming him at times.

He was now married with a 17-year-old son and a great career in engineering ahead of him. However, the peace and contentment seemingly available for him at this point in his life escaped him. Harry, like so many others in life simply refused to let go of the past. Allowing past failures to occupy his mind, they haunted him, causing him to become a prisoner of his past. The past shaped him into the condition of hostility he currently resides in despite his career success. But he was in a hopeful state of mind lately as the CEO of Houston Exponential Engineering (HEE) recently made a surprise announcement - he would be retiring.

Pronouncement would be coming soon on who would be replacing him. Most at the company assumed Harry would be the person to step into the lead position with HEE and he seemed like the most logical choice.

Harry worked side by side with the outgoing CEO on several projects. At times, Harry was the lead person on the project. He was an extremely hardworking and dedicated number two for the CEO. I've "paid my dues" he thought to himself. I've been overlooked my whole life, even by my own father. It's finally my time to fulfill my dreams! Harry said.

The excitement and anticipation of the potential new promotion for Harry appeared to put him in a good place. At least it's what he displayed to those who knew him socially as well as his co-workers. However, secretly his life began to take a darker turn.

A year prior, a chance meeting with a man at the local gym would lead Harry down a path that would have him to question all he thought was good in America. He called himself Rex and he and Harry started getting along almost immediately.

Rex possessed an outgoing and charismatic personality which was the opposite of Harry's, but the two clicked instantly. One day Rex invited Harry out to what he told Harry was an even more exclusive club. "Only for our kind he said, people like you and me!" he said with excitement.

Great sounds good to me Harry said. Believing Rex to be talking about business or professional people and committed to Rex he would certainly attend their next meeting.

Rex, it turns out was a leader of a white supremacist Neo-Nazis group based in SE Texas. They were actively recruiting for more members in the state. Rex saw men like Harry Jacobs, who were leaders in business, law enforcement, or government as essential to the cause of white power and believed Harry could be a part of a growing trend for his people. During the meeting, Harry sat in amazement at the number of people in attendance, especially the number of familiar faces he saw.

Some he noticed from around town, others he knew from his own neighborhood or saw at the local high school picking up their children. Even past school teachers for his son Harry Jr. Harry. He was spellbound by the white nationalist agenda and rhetoric. I guess you can have "fine people" on both sides. Harry laughed to himself.

"I didn't know when you invited me to this meeting what it was" Harry said to Rex afterwards.

"Our movement needs men like you Harry, men in power, men with brains, but able see the bigger picture". "A brighter future" Rex replied to Harry.

What does your movement have to do with me? Harry asked. Everything! Said Rex excitedly.

You told me about some of the hopes and dreams you coveted growing up Harry said Rex seizing on an opportunity. How you always wanted to play football for the Texas Longhorns and were denied the opportunity Rex continued.

Have you noticed how many of those "jungle monkeys"

they have out there playing! Half of the damn team is from Africa. They have stolen your dream, our dreams and look what it has done to your relationship with your father. You haven't spoken to him in years Harry and its all their fault! Their fault? Said Harry in amazement. What do black people have to do with me and my father not speaking said Harry growing emotional about the subject.

Think about it Rex replied. If you had gotten the chance to fulfill your one dream, then you and your dad would probably still be close as ever.

And now there are even more immigrants coming here Harry. "We must do something to preserve our race, preserve our heritage" Rex said to Harry in a commanding tone.

The conversation grew more and more emotional for Harry as Rex started to bring back those old feelings of failure. Pushing the correct buttons was one of the things Rex mastered as a leader and recruiter of his Neo-Nazi group. He was a psychology major in college and well versed in the art of stirring up past emotions to get people to buy in to his point of view. Rex played on Harry's emotions, and brought back those feelings of failure and discontent from past episodes in his life knowing Harry carried them around like baggage. Harry sat there calming himself while Rex sized him up to see what affect he was having on him. He wanted to leave Harry on a positive note.

"And besides Harry, you will soon be the new CEO of HEE INC. what better position for one of us to be in" said Rex. How did you know I was up for the position? Harry asked looking confused. We have our ways said Rex smiling as he left the room.

It was now three months since the CEO of Houston

Exponential Engineering announced he would be stepping down. With still no news yet about who his successor would be. Harry was being summoned before the board of directors. They wanted to share some important news with him prior to making a public announcement. Harry was filled with both anxiety and excitement as he prepared himself for the 2:00 meeting today. This would be the achievement of a lifetime, the fulfillment of a dream, and a day of celebration for Harry. A day of redemption for all the past letdowns and unfulfilled dreams. The news they were about to share with Harry would be life changing.

Almost everyone expected the new CEO position would go to Harry Jacobs. A hardworking and faithful employee. However, Harry received some jarring news in his meeting with the board. "The board has decided to go in a different direction Harry." Said Steven, a longtime board member. Oh, yeah what direction is that? Responded Harry. I know you and a lot of others around here figured you'd be the next in line for the CEO position Steven said. I believe I've earned it! replied Harry in a stern voice. You've done great work around here Harry and have made yourself into a valuable part of the team we've built Steven continued.

But you must trust us on this one Harry, what we are doing now is for the long-term growth and sustainability of the company. The person we were looking for was someone who could lead us to even higher heights. A real leader with critical thinking skills along with outside the box solutions. A person of vision. We realize this must be disappointing news for you Harry and we're sorry, but our decision was unanimous and its also final Steven said in a stern voice. Do you have any questions for the board on this matter Harry? Asked Steven Lawrence.

Harry did not answer he simply sat there in a momentary state of shock and shook his head no. Also, Harry, I know this is short notice but our choice for the position will be in town from Chicago at the end of the week and we'll formally introduce him to the team as the new CEO then.

His name is Conrad James; you'll get the chance to meet him personally. Oh, and by the way before I forget said Steven, you guys are going to be neighbors as well, the company owns other houses on the same block as yours. We gave him one as part of his recruitment package. I think you're going to like him Harry said Steven in a blunt tone. Harry left his meeting and went home for the day feeling numb from the day's developments and angry at the callous way in which it was handled.

CHAPTER 5

The Chosen One

Houston Exponential Engineering was holding a large company meeting at their corporate office in Houston and via video conferencing to their outlets around the world to make one of the biggest announcements in the company's 25-year history - the naming of the new CEO of their global corporation.

While they were outlining some of the details about the background, achievements, and accolades of the new CEO, in walked Conrad James, a tall African American male with an athletic build from a prestigious school and an expert in the little known, but emerging field of Quantum Engineering, Conrad possessed a revolutionary approach to quantum technology.

Conrad always looked confident, sure of himself and in control. From the crowd of over 10,000 HEE employees came a mixture of thunderous applause and gasps from those who could not believe the sight they were witnessing. The first African American CEO at HEE as well as in the field of Quantum Engineering stepped to the podium.

He had a thunderous voice and his timing was always perfect. Conrad captivated the audience as he laid out some of the vision and plans for the company and its thousands of employees worldwide. Some who initially reacted in disapproval, skepticism, or were simply held speechless when Conrad walked in were soon caught up in this skillful orator. It was easy to see why the board of directors chose him over the hundreds of others they were considering. Conrad always stood out from the crowd. Although unique and different in his thinking, he was skilled in communicating his thoughts and connecting with others. Conrad won over most attending the meeting before it was over.

Stepping back from the podium briefly, and taking in the moment of cheers and nods, Conrad's thoughts went back to his mother and all she taught him and encouraged him to do. "She would be so proud to have seen this day come." Conrad said aloud but to himself.

My mom named me Conrad because she always wanted me to be different, to stand out. She'd always say "no one expects to see a black man named Conrad, so they'll never be ready for what you represent." Boy, was she ever right he thought to himself and smiled.

Conrad James had confidently ridden into town and made a lasting first impression on the thousands in attendance. He did not disappoint, delivering the speech of his life in front of the board of directors who felt a wave of relief with the crowd's response. He ended with a wave in the air and a vow to be the CEO for everyone and to move this company to new heights before disappearing from the stage.

The following day Conrad, his wife Janice, and their 18-year old son Jordan were moving into the large home directly across the street from Harry Jacobs and his family. In the Houston suburb of Sun Park, TX. It was a beautiful town with a picturesque look and feel. The streets were lined with Oak and Black Berry trees and the community was the epitome of suburban life in South Eastern Texas. The properties were owned by HEE Inc. and given to their top executives when they came aboard.

The sight of Conrad and his family moving into this community surprised and amazed some of his neighbors. However, they greeted them with genuine warmth and neighborly kindness. All except for the one man who was directly across the street from the James family, Harry Jacobs.

Harry started to experience a burning hatred inside of him at the arrival of the community's first black family and the man who was given the CEO position that was "rightfully his". "Rex was right, this country's going to hell" Harry thought to himself as he peered through a window from his living room facing the new James residence.

Harry had been attending the Neo-Nazis meetings conducted by Rex regularly for about six months now and was teetering back and forth on whether he would commit to formally joining. Now presented with a choice to make, one he believed would be best for his family, his community, even the country, he decided at that moment it was the logical choice to go all in.

Harry was not raised to think and feel this way about African Americans or any other race for that matter. His dad seemed to have plenty of black friends from his football and college days and never expressed anything negative about them in general. The only thing his dad ever told him regarding race was "you will find out there are good people and bad on earth no matter the color. The key is to hang around the good and stay away from the bad regardless of race."

But Rex, the leader of the white supremacist group was skilled at shifting people's focus away from all they had. To place it onto things they believed they didn't have.

Rex first piqued Harry's interest with some of the group's teachings. Now he was becoming one of Harry's closes confidants and someone he considered a friend. Rex had sized up Harry correctly and knew what strings to tug on to get him thinking emotionally about some of his past frustrations, including his failure to "live up to your dad's expectations."

Harry was being lured into the white supremacist group by Rex. He knew how to connect with his issues, and they formed a bond that appeared to be growing day by day.

Harry told his wife Judy about what he was doing and about some of the activities of the group. Judy did not agree with what the Neo-Nazis were spewing out but did not put up much of a fuss about it. In fact, Judy rarely if ever disagreed with Harry and would never do so publicly.

Judy Jacobs was always trained by her mother to be the "good wife" and simply submit to her husband's wishes. Her only concern was to not have the white supremacist beliefs interfere with their "normal family life." Judy witnessed Harry grow more and more angry by the day as he continued to interact and accept the teachings of Neo-Nazism, and their love for Adolf Hitler's teachings.

Harry sat in a daze looking out his living room window at the tall African American man and his family moving in across the street. He instinctively called Rex on the phone and in a casual manner said to Rex. "We need to meet" and hung up the phone.

CHAPTER 6

The Meeting: Choose a side

Rex smiled as he was pulling into the driveway of his new friend and potential recruit Harry Jacobs. It was a moment he was expecting and one he looked forward to with great anticipation. Rex said to himself while still in the car "I knew this day was coming it's all going as planned."

Rex was well connected in the business world and knew beforehand Harry Jacobs would not be getting the position of CEO of HEE Inc. Rex was playing coy in their previous conversation where he said to Harry, he believed he would get the CEO position. He simply wanted to increase Harry's level of expectation of getting the job, saying to himself "with greater expectations comes greater disappointment."

Rex the "psychologist" was simply playing the game, pulling strings on the somewhat naïve Harry. Rex knew of Harry's need to belong to something.

Not being a part of the football team as a youth, the setback of not making the high school team and not living up to his dad's expectations caused him to become engulfed by a "spirit of rejection" which he brought into all his relationships.

As he was stepping out of the car, Rex said to himself "Harry's yearning to belong to something, his disenchantments and feelings of rejection were fertile ground for our Neo-Nazi and white supremacist teachings, it's time to close the deal".

By the time Rex walked through the front door of Harry's home he could see Harry was seething in a fit of rage.

What's the problem Harry? Rex said feigning not to already

know.

You were right Rex! You were right all along, and I should have listened to you Harry said. Right about what? said Rex.

"Those niggers, those immigrants they are here to take our jobs, our way of life from us" Harry shouted. Calm down for a moment. Rex said. Are we alone? Yes, replied Harry.

I should have known this would happen. It seems like I always get the short end of the stick shouted Harry who was now talking at the top of his voice. All the bitterness of the past allowed to fester in his heart and mind, seized the opportunity and now controlled him.

What happened Harry Rex repeated. I didn't get the CEO position after all said Harry with contempt in his voice! All my hard work, all the dedication I've shown to this company and to get passed over once again, this is the last straw. To make matters worse, they gave the position to one of those niggers you've been telling me about! I'll bet it must have been through some type of quota or minority affirmative action program Harry continued as the anger in his voice grew with every word. The room was thick with emotion and intensity. What an unfair advantage these people are given over us! Harry shouted.

Rex smiled seeing Harry was listening to the rhetoric he's been teaching in their meetings then he chimed in. That's what I've been telling you Harry.

We must continue to do all we can to draw attention to the "plight of the white man in America." We are being treated very unfairly in our own country. We built this country Harry. Don't you see? These immigrants are the cause of all of America's problems. They're just here to take, take, and take and not give anything back. Soon it will be more of them than us if we don't do something. They want to replace us said Rex stirring the pot and in full speech mode.

Can I count on you Harry? Are you now ready to fully commit to joining us, to helping the cause of the white man in America? Will you commit to helping your own people regain what is rightfully theirs? It's our heritage, our birthright Harry and God wants us to do something! Rex was now on a roll, closing the deal.

Harry peeped through his living room window and could see Conrad James, his wife, and son still carrying small boxes into the house across the street. I'm all in said Harry.

Look they are even taking over the block where we've made our home said Harry pointing at the James family. I'm ready to do whatever is necessary to take back our country.

Great! Replied Rex, besides, I already have a position in mind for you.

You will be our new CEO of online content, activity, and recruitment. You will have the crucial responsibility of bringing into our movement a new breed of young whites. Men and women who can help keep the vision alive well into the future!

With your engineering background, tech skills and the broad reach we can now have on the internet, you are the perfect fit for the position Harry said Rex emphatically.

As Rex was preparing to leave, he glanced out the window and saw Conrad James. What's his specialty? What skills do he bring to the table to be given the position over you? Rex asked pointing with contempt at Conrad.

Quantum Engineering replied Harry. Rex paused in amazement. "How'd that nigger get a mind like that" said Rex on his way out the door.

Chapter 7

Choosing to Continue down the Wrong Path

Six months after Paul Wilson and Andre Jackson took over the leadership of WKROC TV news in Houston, their plans to make it the number one news channel in the city of Houston and all Southeastern Texas was producing the results Paul Wilson anticipated. Andre as News Director managed all content and day to day operations for the station. He directed all the on-air personalities to follow the script he and Paul discussed.

"We need to constantly bombard the public with negative images of black and brown people to compete in this market for media ratings. That is how we get ahead in today's media market."

Paul demanded a commitment to his plan from Andre as a condition for him being elevated to News Director. During the intense meeting six months ago, they almost came to blows, but they managed to recover and reconcile their differences. Paul convinced Andre to look at the "bigger picture" he called it, so they could do what was best for the station and themselves.

Whatever initial feelings of reluctance Andre experienced in the beginning now took a back seat to his career advancement goals and personal priorities. Ratings, ratings, ratings were the name of the game.

Things started off bumpy for Andre as he worked to implement the new strategy with his news anchors and the staff at the station but Andre's type A personality allowed him to be very persuasive when he needed to be. He now had the authority to get things done. Although the news anchors didn't like it or agree, they decided to go along to save their jobs and hopefully the station from the direction it was being moved in by Paul and Andre.

Pricilla Prescott was the lead anchor of the two-person morning news team, the highest rated show among all the station's programing.

Pricilla called Andre to set up a meeting to talk about some "important issues" she wanted to discuss with him. Walking into her News Director's office she sat down abruptly and obviously bothered.

Something seems to be bothering you Pricilla; is everything ok? Andre asked knowing the answer.

I've come to talk to you about the direction you and Paul are taking this station in as well as my role in it said Pricilla. What seems to be the problem? Replied Andre.

What's the problem? She narrowed her eyes and looked at him in surprise. It's racist and un-American for starters that's what the problem is said Pricilla forcefully.

How so? said Andre.

All we do is stoke fear and division in our news now. There is less of an emphasis on the facts involved and it seems we are only catering to certain segments of society Pricilla said adamantly. You only ok content that is derogatory towards African Americans, Hispanics and immigrants and you expect us to continue repeating the information and showing negative images constantly.

Not so said Andre. We are reporting the news and giving the public what it wants. I don't know if you've noticed

Pricilla, but your show is the number one show in Houston, even Southeastern Texas Andre said trying to convince Pricilla.

Pricilla jumped in. "I've been wrestling between this job and my conscience for months now. I came here to do the news. I'm a journalist not a talk show host!" Pricilla continued. Those "opinion reporters" are nothing more than entertainers and I don't want to become one of them. I don't think in good conscience I can continue in this job. Pricilla said.

Now hold on a minute Pricilla. Just give us a little time and once we make this station all Paul and I have envisioned, I promise you will be more than happy with the work we're doing for the community.

I'm not the only one who feels this way Andre. Just listen to this vague description you ok'd for the last white suspect who was a danger to the city said Pricilla. *"Six ft. tall, medium build, medium complexion wearing dark clothing and a hat.* Pricilla read verbatim from a sheet of paper she used on-air.

Nobody can tell who that is from such a general and vague description. There is not even a mention of the ethnicity of the person. The fact is Andre, he is white! We have a very good sketch of the person as well and never showed it, and to top it off, we pushed it to the end of the time slot.

All the minority descriptions are extremely specific and accurate and we show a picture of the suspect whenever possible and run it multiple times a day. Why is that? All this does is create hysteria and negative stereotypes said Pricilla emphatically.

Andre saw a moment where he could jump in and give his response to Pricilla's concerns." I agreed to meet with you on this matter because of the respect we have for you and the great job you are doing to help make WKROC the number one station in Houston.

As our number one anchor, you deserve a certain level of respect. However, our decision on the direction of the station is final Andre said decisively. You have to trust us Pricilla we're doing what's best for everyone.

How can you of all people, a black man, be in support of this Andre? I'm shocked said Pricilla with a painful expression on her face.

Because I understand the "bigger picture" Pricilla. This is a ratings game!

They went back and forth for another five minutes before coming to a halt as their emotions were rising with each passing minute.

Pricilla then stated firmly, "when the public is at risk, I won't be a part of covering up the facts. Not for you Andre, Paul or for WKROC." The news is the news if people want to be entertained then they have other options.

We've experienced several mass shootings here in the state of Texas. This is my home state and I won't participate in putting this great state at risk.

What do you mean asked Andre?

After the last mass shooting you directed us to pursue and keep pushing this mental illness angle with the suspects involved simply because they were white suburban kids I suspect said Pricilla. Andre did not respond.

Evilness is not a mental illness she said. Then pausing for a moment for emphasis she added - It's a spiritual sickness! Just remember Andre, we're all only one person away from knowing someone who has been victimized by the senseless gun violence that is plaguing our country. Pricilla said as she walked out of his office.

Chapter 8

The High Cost of Choosing to Do Nothing

The same day, another meeting was taking place. Despite their reluctance, Oliver Jones and Henry Allen met again with the principal of Sun Park High School regarding the abuse. Mr. Watters promised the boys they were doing all they could to stop them from being bullied by the younger Fletcher and his friends. I have been assured by the Fletcher family the teasing was all in fun. Nevertheless, Mr. Watters stated, "I will speak to Mr. Fletcher personally on this matter to get to the bottom of it."

Although the principal acted as if he was concerned, about the abuse the kids were enduring at the school. The subject had not gone over well. He did not want to take on an issue he believed might smear the name of the school. Besides, Sun Park High School was in the middle of its fundraising season and its principal, Frank Watters, did not want to blemish the school's reputation during this critical time.

Mr. Watters traveled throughout the state of Texas highlighting the campus's extravagant new Howard Fletcher Technology center to the governor, state senators and business leaders.

Although he knew he had to at least discuss this situation, he was very clear I do not want to see any negative news get out regarding "my school", he declared to an associate.

Principal Watters was a guest at the Fletcher family home for social functions on many occasions. The Fletcher home was a place where the who's who of the area came together for both socializing and business. They were having one such party tonight.

This evening, he had to at least bring up the issues Oliver and Henry were having and did so between sips of his drink as they sat around drinking and laughing at a party that night. "Boys will be boys" said Howard Fletcher to Mr. Watters with a tip of his glass. They both shrugged and laughed it off, minimizing the seriousness of the mistreatment. I'll speak to the boys, continued Mr. Fletcher. Both men in positions of authority chose to not use it to deal with the problem for the sake of their image.

The conversation between Howard Fletcher Sr. and his son Howard Jr. displaying a lack of accountability and discipline from the father. Launched his son and their online group into their extreme escalation of cyberbullying Oliver and Henry. Later in the evening the boys received over 200 messages in their inboxes online. The following day the number rose to 1500, then 5900 the next day, from there 18000, and by the end of the week, the boys were receiving over 30,000 messages a day from bully's all over the world.

The group had now tapped into the power of the internet and this exposed a darkness in people. A crowd like mentality that will incite others to jump into the next "popularity game". Luring them to participate in mercilessly attacking any individual to be a part of the "in-crowd".

The privacy of being at home or on a personal cell phone, the false sense of security of feeling safe from exposure, and the temptations of the internet can reveal a lot about the condition of the heart of people. Conditions ripe for festering a mob mentality.

Cyberbullying, like other vices, allows people to display evilness and cruelty from the "comfort" of their own homes.

Not even the younger Fletcher could have imagined the exponential growth of his online terror group. Not only was the group gaining large numbers, but also the nastiness was increasing in intensity. People jumped in attempting to show higher levels of cruelty than the last one. Teenagers seeking popularity, looking to fit in and belong to something or some with their own low self-esteem issues sought refuge in the misery of Oliver and Henry. The same held true for the adults who followed the crowd.

The reward bounty money they raised from the first day of school was now well over $5,000 and the bounty, as well as the online bullying, created a "buzz" around the school. As the boys walked from classroom to classroom, they were the subjects of jeers, finger pointing, and taunts from their classmates most of whom they had never met before. They were also being ignored by people who once appeared to be their friends but now avoided them afraid they would become targets themselves.

Activities typical school age children look forward to having like lunch breaks became unbearable. The intensity of the tormenting was magnified during those times. By Friday of the first week of the school year the boy's pictures were plastered all over the internet. They were now the targets of an incessant and relentless bullying campaign.

Oliver Jones and Henry Allen had always kept a standing appointment with one another. Although unspoken it became customary for the two boys to meetup at Henry's house on Saturday mornings and hang out together. Henry's parents would always be gone on weekends running errands or on vacation, so it was a perfect time of bonding and friendship for them. But this time was different. With the end of the first week of school complete and the onslaught of harassment they were being subjected to, Oliver knew this time would not be the same.

Oliver was aware Henry previously needed some mental health counseling from the harassment the boys received in prior years. However, Oliver realized the intensity of the mistreatment now reached a level unmatched before. Walking briskly to the front door of his best friend's house he felt a sense of urgency as he rang the doorbell and simply walked inside. Letting himself in just as had done so many times before. There was an ominous feeling in the air as if danger loomed. Oliver walked with a quick pace, urgently, hurried, wanting to check on his best friend in light of the escalating magnitude of the cyberbullying they were experiencing and Henry's history of needing mental health counseling.

As he entered his best friend's bedroom, he found him sprawled out on the floor. The room was dark, shades drawn to block all sunlight and Henry's eyes pointed up at the ceiling blankly, looking as if he were in a daze. His face looked pale, his appearance was untidy and in disarray looking as if he had not changed clothing or showered in a few days. Previously crying, but not now he was all out of tears, Henry obviously was planted in that position for hours.

Oliver called out to his friend. Henry, Henry! He shouted. Henry, Henry! Oliver shouted again still getting no answer. Are you ok? How long have you been lying there on the floor like this? He asked. Henry finally turned his eyes towards his best friend. I want to die Oliver; I want to kill myself Henry stated flatly. Stop all your crazy talk said Oliver. Everything is going to be all right; we are going to get through this together.

I can't go on any longer said Henry. I feel hopeless, lonely and ashamed. There is no escaping this constant tormenting Henry said as his phone constantly pinged in the background signifying the relentless inbox messages, texts, and calls he received from bully's who joined forces with Howard Fletcher's group.

Why don't you just turn off your phone and stay off the internet asked Oliver. I wanted to but I also need to reach my mom and I did not want them to win, it makes me feel like a victim and besides, I wanted to prove I could handle things myself, just this once replied Henry.

I understand. I'm at my wits end with these people myself and I refuse to run from them anymore. Said Oliver. Henry sat up for a minute and said "this on-line bullying is the worst; I'd much rather be physically bullied, face to face. At least it comes to an end after a few minutes. People are drawn to cruelty these days. They admire nastiness".

They both just sat there in silence for about an hour. Oliver who could have a temper problem from time to time was now burning in a silent rage. He also did not want to involve his mother after their recent move to Sun Park, TX and the death of his father due to a drunk driving accident. However, he felt more anger for what they did to his friend Henry than for himself. "I can handle these punks Oliver said defiantly to himself.

As they sat together in the dark, Oliver's mood became gloomy, more ominous, shifting from sadness to anger to rage and from rage to hatred and finally to thoughts of revenge. "One day we're going to make them pay Henry, we're going to make them all pay!" Oliver said.

Chapter 9

Family Choices

It had now been a couple of weeks since Conrad, Janice, and Jordan became fulltime residents of Sun Park, TX. On a typically quiet evening the family was sitting down to dinner discussing how the relocation was going. I know this area is a bit different from Chicago, but it is beautiful down here said Conrad attempting to start a conversation.

I love it here in Texas Janice replied with excitement. Now I understand what people mean when they talk about southern hospitality. These are some of the nicest people I've ever met. I'm getting used to this way of life already - I love the southern charm She added with a smile.

All the neighbors have stopped by to say hello and brought some type of gift, except for the couple across the street. They seem like private people.

Conrad and Janice were going back and forth about the virtues of southern living and the great Texas traditions they were experiencing when they noticed that Jordan had not said a word. What's going on son? Is everything ok with you? How's football practice going? Conrad rattled off quickly.

Everything is fine said Jordan and football is great. You were right Dad, the level of competition for Texas high school football is more intense and so is the coaching. I need to focus a lot more on my technique and the fundamentals, but it's ok, it's good for me. Jordan added.

You are teammates with the kid across the street Harry Jacobs Jr. right, doesn't he play for Sun Park? asked

Conrad. Yeah, he's the quarterback Dad Jordan said dryly; but we don't talk much. Why not son if he's the quarterback? You're a wide receiver you guys are going to have to communicate. He throws the ball and you catch the ball, I expect you'll be the best of buddies soon said Conrad laughing.

I don't think so Dad, Jordan said in a low tone. Hey, maybe you two can walk to school together and walk back home together Janice offered with her usual enthusiasm. Nah, I'm good said Jordan without looking up.

Conrad and Janice looked at one another in a confused way. Are we missing something son? What seems to be the problem? Conrad asked. He's a damn racist redneck and I wouldn't cross the street with him replied Jordan and stormed out of the room leaving his parents with stunned looks on their faces.

At that precise moment, directly across the street another family was sitting down to evening dinner. At the home of Harry and Judy Jacobs the family gathered for their traditional evening dinner where Harry loved to talk football with his son Harry Jr., now a star quarterback for Sun Park High School, as well as the day's events at work or on the local news.

Harry usually dominated the conversation with his wife Judy spending most of her time agreeing with Harry's opinions. Never one to make waves, Judy enjoyed being "the good wife" in the background for Harry. Harry Jr. always admired his dad and respected his opinions.

Harry's mood recently appeared to be growing darker and darker since his displeasure over not getting the CEO position he coveted. That singular event seemed to bring back all of Harry's old feelings of rejection from his dad.

Harry, felt he was not living up to his dad's expectations of him by not playing football at the University of Texas and becoming a professional football player like he was and his grandfather before him. Harry never got over the emotion of rejection, it consumed him.

Oftentimes his emotions submerged him into a state of disillusionment over his life. And now not being able to fulfill his goal of "showing his dad" he could still be somebody and not being named CEO of a major corporation brought all the pent-up emotion back to the surface, weighing Harry down.

The past was once again dictating both his present and future as Harry often allowed past hurts to linger in his heart and mind. They effected his decision making, work, and family life. The heavy burdens chased him down from behind, dominating his thoughts continually and dictating his current mood.

Despite having a family, beautiful home, material success, and a potentially bright future with HEE Inc, Harry was frequently a prisoner of his past.

Harry choices started to have a greater effect on his family. He decided to become a full member of his white supremacist group resulting in him sinking deeper and deeper into hatred for blacks, Jews, and Hispanics.

"All these immigrants are making this country fall apart! Stated Harry with emotion. I can't believe we now have a family of niggers living right across the street from us" Harry continued.

Do you have to talk like that at dinner and in front of our son? Judy asked in her usual low tone. The boy needs to hear the truth. Said Harry.

Listen son, these fucking Jews are trying to take over our

country, and the niggers and immigrants just want free hand outs. "Pass me the butter Judy." Harry said casually revealing a new level of comfort in his hate speech. That's the reason I've made the choices I have for us son, for our country you understand! Yes, Sir, Pop replied Harry Jr.

I should have been the CEO of HEE Inc., do you know how big it would have been for us, what it could have done for our family? Harry said almost to himself as the atmosphere grew dark throughout the house.

   The conversations led by Harry recently would often lead the family to a point of mental anguish, sadness, and dejection. Harry's lost sense of reality now broke through their plush suburban lifestyle. For despite, all they enjoyed, Harry's belief of his dream being stolen, his last shot at validation falling short created an air of gloom throughout the house.

   How can you be so angry about life Harry said Judy timidly? How, can you not be satisfied or content with your life? we have everything we need and more Judy continued.

Not everything! Harry replied. That nigger across the street has my job! Harry said with contempt holding on tight to his failure. These types of conversations started to happen with more frequency as Harry's Neo-Nazi beliefs grew more and more radical.

   Later Harry decided he would settle in for the evening. He poured himself a shot of liquor and sat back in his favorite chair in front of the television to watch the evening news. After the first shot, he poured a second, and then a third. He felt content now, relaxed as he watched his chosen television news channel.

   WKROC the number one news channel in the city of

Houston was always on when Harry was home. They quickly became his favorite place for news because they always affirmed his personal biases and prejudices towards people of other nationalities. "That's exactly what Rex has been talking about, got damn illegals" Harry shouted shaking his head. This in response to a story highlighting some of the negative stereotypes of "illegal immigrants". "Send them back to where they came from" Harry muttered to himself while sitting there alone in the dark.

Chapter 10

Face to Face with Choice

Under the dynamic leadership of Conrad James at HEE Inc., the company's stock price increased by a record 50% in six months. Conrad was a visionary thinker, with cutting edge ability to generate solutions. He also possessed great people skills with the ability to command a room with his presence. The company was moving forward with his bold thinking and initiatives due to his Quantum Engineering background and skills. HEE Inc. became the company to partner with for business, technological, and engineering solutions.

HEE Inc. obtained several new contracts in a short amount of time. Other organizations were anxious to tap into the abilities the emerging young CEO brought to the table. The influx of new contracts started coming in from not only other corporations but also government agencies, nonprofits, even world health and food organizations. Everyone wanted to see how the technology of Quantum Engineering could help them develop their technological programs and drive solutions.

Despite this early success, Conrad was aware there might be a potential problem looming over the company and he wanted to meet the challenge directly. Conrad saw it as a hidden crack in the armor which could be damaging to the entire company. He wanted to seal it and not wait for it to sneak up on him. He asked his Assistant to setup a meeting with one of his senior VP's so they could get things straighten out. She called Harry Jacobs to arrange a meeting.

Conrad and his wife Janice engaged in a long

conversation with their son Jordan after he made the comment about Harry Jr. being a racist. Conrad assured Jordan that "if you simply kept God first, worked hard, and made good choices in life there was nothing anyone could do to stop you no matter what they believed." But now was the time he and Harry needed to meet to air out any potential differences. To be sure they could have a good working relationship.

Conrad was impressed with the work of Harry Jacobs, but was not going to allow him to poison the atmosphere they were creating at Houston Exponential Engineering Inc.

Harry dreaded having to take a meeting at the request of Conrad James his new, but unwanted neighbor and boss. He was tempted to go home sick, but then he said to himself. "I may as well get this over with, it's bound to happen eventually. I can't believe I have to report to this nigger" he said in disgust.

Harry walked into the office of Conrad with purpose, business like, intentionally being sure not to smile.

Good afternoon said Conrad as Harry walked into his office. How can I help you? Replied Harry in a monotone voice. Harry was the last of the six VP's at the company to meet with Conrad and thought to be the favorite to become the new CEO.

Conrad attempted to break the ice with a few personal questions. How's your wife and family Harry? Your son plays on the same team with my son at Sun Park High School and I hear he's one of the top players in the state. You must be really proud of him huh Harry? How long have you been living in the community of Sun Park it seems like a great place to raise a family. Conrad rattled off.

I'd rather talk only about business if you don't mind Harry replied in a businesslike manner.

"I've been reviewing your work Harry and it looks like you and your department do some good work down there" Conrad said." Yeah well I know what I'm doing I've been doing this for a while now" Said Harry. "No one has ever given me anything" Harry said with emphasis.

Great Harry, making money the old-fashioned way huh? Conrad said half joking.

    Can I be honest with you Harry stated.   I'm not going to be hanging out with "your kind" or inviting you over to my house or anything. I'm just here to do my job is that going to be a problem? Harry asked firmly both unable and unwilling to hide his disgust at having to report to the younger and darker skinned Conrad James.

Not for me replied Conrad calmly sensing the type of man Harry was. But can you tell me who "my kind is?" Conrad asked. I'd rather keep my personal opinions to myself Harry said. Personal opinions? You've never met me before replied Conrad so please feel free to enlighten me about who "my kind" is.

Although they both were speaking in a controlled manner it did not prevent the atmosphere from being filled with friction.

    A moment of awkwardness followed as the two men sized one another up, anticipating the next moment. It was like high stakes poker between them. You already know what it means Harry finally answered. It must be nice to be able to stumble into a position at such a young age, to be given every advantage over good hardworking people said Harry as hostilities began to rise even higher.

    I must be missing something can you be more specific

asked Conrad as he sensed Harry was getting angry.

Sure, since you asked Harry answered. "I didn't receive any affirmative action or government set asides to get to where I am. I've worked for everything I've gotten my whole life", that's what "real Americans" do! Emotion finally showing in his voice.

Didn't your dad and granddad play for the University of Texas football team and in the NFL for 10 years? They're both famous men down here in Texas and I hear wealthy men as well Conrad pointed out. Harry didn't respond. Why didn't you follow in their footsteps and play football Harry? Conrad asked.

I didn't get the opportunity to play there, I wasn't gifted like you I guess said Harry sarcastically.

"So, you believe I've been given advantages in life huh Harry?" Conrad asked with a look of disbelief on his face.

You carry around not playing football at UT like your father and grandfather did like a weight and from meeting you I'm guessing you are still upset about it. I can sense a heavy burden you've placed upon yourself. You may not have played college football, but you've always known you were going to college. It was expected of you from birth in fact. Conrad continued.

Growing up in Henry Horner Projects in Chicago I didn't even know a person who had ever gone to college. I didn't know anyone who had a job paying them a livable wage, or even anyone who owned a car for that matter. Things you took for granted growing up I could have been killed for having where I lived.

On my college application, they asked for three professional references. The only people I knew with jobs at the time were the lady Janitor of the building whose son I grew up with. The maintenance man at Crane High School who lived in my building, and Mr. Major Adams who ran the Henry Horner Boys Club. Those were the people I used on my college application and I was honored to be able to do so.

Is that about it boss Harry said with a hint of disdain in his voice not wanting to hear anything that contradicted his personal beliefs. So, do you think you can work with "my kind" Conrad asked. You'll have my reports each month, any other communications can be through email or my Assistant Harry said.

Conrad wanted to bring the meeting to a close by addressing the biggest issue. There's one other thing Harry. I've heard some talk about some of your extracurricular activities, some of your online presence Conrad stated. There's talk about you being lured into some of those hate groups, white supremacist, or Neo-Nazis Conrad said bluntly.

So, you believe you're some type of victim huh Harry? That's where you get all your "poor white man in America" talk I'm sure. You guys must be delusional. Conrad said shaking his head.

Is there anything in the company policy specifically against it? Harry asked already knowing the answer. The policy is to respect all races, treat everyone fairly, and have equal opportunities for all people.

Doesn't that sound American Harry. Conrad said. If you do anything to reflect badly on this company, I'm going to act Harry. Harry Jacobs smiled as he turned to walk away. Your day is coming nigger! He muttered to himself on his way out the door.

Chapter 11

The same bad choice again, and again, and again!

Andre Jackson sat alone inside of his office for a couple of hours. It was a time of reflection and self-examination. The meeting he held earlier in the day with his number one news anchor Pricilla Prescott left a lasting impression on him and he was now deep in thought, feeling regretful. Andre was wondering if he was doing the right thing by helping Paul Wilson take WKROC news in the direction the station was heading.

He realized what they were doing was exploiting racial stereotypes, capitalizing on America's racial, economic, and political divisions but Paul made a convincing argument for him to "look at the bigger picture" Paul called it. As he sat pondering the conversation, Pricilla's words resonated even more deeply, especially her parting words. "Just remember Andre, we're all only one person away from knowing someone who has been victimized by the senseless gun violence in our country."

Today was the day the news ratings would be announced for local television stations along with several individual journalism awards. WKROC TV station already had planned a huge celebration party for later in the evening in anticipation of winning several honors. However, at the moment all Andre could think about were the words of Pricilla, who stirred up something in his conscience that would not allow him to prepare for the big day.

Andre walked over to the office of his station General Manager and mentor Paul Wilson unannounced. There was a sense of urgency about him. We need to talk Andre said to Paul upon entering. Ok what's on your mind Andre you look bothered by something?

I'm starting to receive some pushback on what we've been doing around here Paul, the direction that we've taken the station in. This emphasis on minorities and immigrants when it comes to reporting the news. Andre answered. Yeah? But look at the ratings we've been receiving. The station's viewership is way up from last year Paul said.

Great Paul, but I'm starting to believe it's not worth it. Talking to Pricilla has me thinking about the potential damage we could be causing long term Andre responded.

Pricilla! That's her one flaw as a journalist Andre. She's driven too much by her conscience Paul laughingly said attempting lighten the moment. Tonight, we are going to be named the number one station for news in Houston and SE Texas and I have already set up the party and entertainment for this evening. Paul added.

At what cost though Paul, all we're doing is exploiting racism and divisions for the sake of ratings Andre said with his voice getting louder and the room temperature rising. Now don't go getting a conscience on me Andre, you sound like Pricilla Paul interjected. We are almost there, where we want to be. Remember the plan. Let's stick to it.

"I know it's racism, but it's institutional racism and almost impossible to prove Paul said. Remember what I told you about institutional racism? Not only is it harder to prove, it can't be quantified.

No one can say this or that happened to me because of institutional racism, it doesn't hurt anyone directly, it only protects the status quo! Paul said with emphasis. But what if it's the status quo that hurts people Paul? Andre asked.

I'm starting to believe institutional racism although much harder to prove, is more harmful than the KKK will ever be. It affects a lot more people than individual racism ever has because it works against the progress of a people, against the conscience of a country Andre said standing to his feet. Pricilla may be on to something.

Some people are compelled to participate in the system because of their jobs or service, others participate without even their own knowledge of it. However, systematic racism would not be possible without the complicity, and silent agreement of the "good people" who nonchalantly allow it to flourish.

The bottom line is only those at the very top benefit from institutional racism. The rest of us are being duped by the system, both black and white people.

Those at the top profit off America's divisiveness.

Both Andre and Paul sat in silence for a moment bringing needed calm back to the room, thinking about what was said. Finally, Paul said - I wasn't going to tell you this in advance, I didn't want to spoil the surprise. However, you seem to be a little down right now and could use some encouraging. Tonight, you are going to win the best news executive of the year award and this in your first year! How about that Andre?

It's like I said, you have to look at the bigger picture and one day you'll be in a position of influence and positioned to create change.

Now go home and get yourself ready Andre this is going to be our biggest night of the year.

After Andre left his office Paul immediately picked up the phone and called Rex, his white supremacist group leader.

Everything is going as planned. Paul said. Having one of those niggers do our bidding for us was a brilliant idea on your part. Like you said "all we have to do is offer one of them a position or a little power and they'll work harder against their own people than we are." Paul said.

Some of them are so desperate to be accepted by white people they'll turn on their own kind for a job. He actually believes that I'm his friend and care about his lowly people. Paul continued, they both laughed hysterically at their manipulation before hanging up the phone.

As Andre was driving home to get ready for the banquet, he was still deep in thought. He couldn't stop thinking about some of the words from his mentor and boss Paul Wilson which led him to his choices. *Continue to push minority stereotypes. Continue to bombard the public with black and brown faces whenever there is a crime committed, especially if it's a high-profile crime.* Then we can h*ighlight their arrest and capture for heighten exposure."* These were the conditions attached to the News Director position being offered to him.

Arriving home, Andre was met at the door by his wife Daphne just getting home from work herself after picking up their six-year-old daughter Renae from a neighbor's house. Daphne knew immediately Andre was troubled.

Andre went over with Daphne in "confession style" the conversations with Paul and Priscilla. He then attempted to justify his choices with Daphne but she would have none of it. She believed he should resign from the station immediately. "You're a talented and educated man Andre you can find another job and I'll hold things down until you do" Daphne said.

Andre tried again to convince Daphne otherwise, this time using some of the same reasoning Paul used on him. You have to look at the "bigger picture" Daphne Andre said. I need to be on the inside to change things. Once I'm in a position of power I can then have the influence needed to bring about change within the industry Daphne.

Daphne looked at him for a second then responded. I understand this is a big night for you and WKROC News with the ratings coming out and your banquet tonight and I'll be meeting you at the banquet like we planned. However, you don't need to have a title, position, or award to have influence Daphne said. She kissed him softly on the forehead and left the room to get ready.

Chapter 12

Bad choices, Bad consequences

Dominating the news was a series of burglaries in the Houston area which had the city on edge due to the brazen nature of the suspect. WKROC TV News continued the practice implemented by its News Director Andre Jackson giving the public general and bland descriptions of white suspects when it came to news reports as well as reporting them at the end when many had stopped listening.

The night of the huge celebration for WKROC News career criminal, Avery Wright was inside of a local convenience store not far from the home of Andre Jackson. The police gave all the local news stations detailed descriptions and a sketch of what the suspect looked like which was not included in WKROC's watered down descriptions per Andre's instructions. While at the counter to purchase a six pack of beer Avery Wright noticed two uniformed policemen entered the store. They were now standing directly behind him. There were in fact six people total in line.

Avery Wright, started to feel nervous, edgy and his nervousness caused his heart to flutter. This was often the case when he was in the presence of policemen. Avery possessed the mindset of a criminal, he was always on the lookout to commit a crime, always looking for his next crime victim, on alert for any opportunity.

The close proximity he now occupied with the two policemen forced his mind to race, wondering if they were there for him. Am I finally caught? He thought. It was only a few seconds, but it seemed like time was standing still for Avery.

Suddenly, News Station WKROC broke through the awkward silence. There was an update coming over the television station on a burglary last night along with a description of the suspect. The news anchor gave this vague description. "Male about 6 ft. tall, medium build, medium complexion, wearing a hat, and dark clothing."

The police gave the local stations in the area this description "a white male, 6ft tall, 185 lbs., blonde hair, green eyes, a scar on his left check, tattoos of a snake on both arms". These details were all visibly obvious to see on Avery as he stood at the counter to make his purchase. His heart dashed, his eyes darted left to right as he mentally searched for his getaway exit. A drop of sweat started to roll down his forehead as anxiety rose in his mind. "Should I make a run for it?" Avery thought to himself.

However, the description given out by the news station did nothing to move anyone into any kind of action. It was such a generic description some of the people in line laughed about it, a couple of guys in the back were heard saying that could be anyone of us.

Avery Wright after paying moved intently towards the exit and out the door. Once around the corner, he bolted.

One of the policemen, Officer Eric Kemp became suspicious of the mannerisms of the man inside the store who was standing right in front of them. Thinking to himself, "something was not right with this guy." He hurriedly went to the squad car and asked dispatch to send them a description of the burglary suspect. It came back as a perfect match for Avery. However, by the time they received it he had disappeared fearing they may be checking up on him. Damn! Said Officer Kemp.

Avery Wright felt a sense of relief. Believing he escaped

yet another jam and now emboldened by feelings of invincibility.

Crime was a lifestyle for him, a chosen path with no thoughts of him giving up on his criminal activities. As he drove around the corner of what looked to be a quiet neighborhood, he couldn't help but notice a well-dressed black man who was walking out the front door of his home.

Andre Jackson was leaving for the banquet celebration with his co-workers at WKROC News. His wife Daphne and their daughter Renae left a couple of minutes prior to him so the house immediately went dark as Andre made his way to his car. Avery, sensing a potential opportunity parked a few hundred feet away now watching, scanning the area.

Perfect! Avery said to himself with excitement ringing from his voice. To him this was like having a real job, or a business opportunity presented to him and one he could not pass up. Andre did have a security system in his house but in his rush to make it to the banquet he neglected to activate it.

Avery made his move. He'd done this many times before so within one minute he was already inside of the house.

Avery kept a gun on him but he always told himself it was just for protection. He never wanted to hurt anyone. Avery was inside the house for a couple of minutes when a side door abruptly swung open.

Avery was startled by the noise, scared, and was caught completely off guard. Daphne Jackson forgot the gift she brought for Andre in recognition of his promotion and his career success and she was going to present it to him at the banquet.

Daphne turned on the lights, Avery's heart pounded and

he panicked. Daphne's eye's met Avery's just as he turned and fired one single shot! The bullet struck Daphne right in the heart killing her instantly. Her daughter Renae who was trailing behind her screamed loudly and seeing the face of Avery standing there in a daze she turned and ran towards the side exit door. Avery instinctively fired another shot hitting Renae in the back and she tumbled to the floor. Avery then ran out the same door heading towards his car attempting to flee when two police cars came up the street and blocked his way.

A neighbor saw him enter the house and had already called the police. Avery was apprehended, but not before he had done the unthinkable. The Sun Park community would never be the same again after this tragic filled weekend.

Chapter 13

The Right Choice over the Popular Choice

During this extraordinary week in Sun Park, TX. the high school football team was heading into the playoffs for the Texas state championship. They featured two of the top high school recruits in the country in Harry Jacobs Jr. and Jordan James. The two young men started off the year as bitter enemies of one another. Resulting from the burden of the rivalry that formed between their fathers being passed down to their children.

Jordan was a new transfer from the Chicago area and would have to earn his way onto the team and the respect of his teammates while Harry Jr. was already a top player and personality around the school.

The venom of racial hatred Harry Sr. exposed his son to continually at home affected Harry Jr. He held some of the same racial hatred and stereotypes of his father, causing him and Jordan to collide almost instantly as they made their way onto the football field for practice on the first day.

Being a top high school quarterback made Harry a popular student around town and he and a group of his friends shunned Jordan from the beginning at practice and in the classrooms.

This caused Jordan to have an equal amount of disdain for Harry. However, Jordan and Harry both kept working on the field and remained composed enough to form a working relationship which allowed them to overcome their personal bias and get to know one another. They in fact had no choice as Harry was the quarterback and Jordan earned a spot as the starting wide receiver.

Two events off the field changed the direction of their relationship. The first was a time when Harry Jr. and one of his friends were hanging out at a local pizza shop. A rival high school team noticed them and started to make trouble for them wanting to initiate a confrontation. Outnumbered five to two Harry had no idea what he would do when suddenly Jordan and three of his friends appeared from another portion of the restaurant to have Harry's back and the other group instantly backed down.

Later the same week Harry's car broke down and he was stranded on the side of the road. He neglected to charge up his phone before leaving and was attempting to flag down help. After being passed up by numerous others Jordan happened to be passing by. He noticed Harry and pulled over to help him, giving him a ride home and use of his cell phone. These two incidents caused Harry Jr. to rethink some of his preconceived notions about Jordan and black people in general.

However, Harry ultimately was persuaded to change his beliefs by what he saw from Jordan in the classroom. Harry was at the top of his class academically; he only took honors courses which were reserved for students with the highest test scores. When Jordan was moved into those same courses because of his grades Harry was stunned. Jordan became the second ranked student in the class only behind Harry. He had believed all the Neo-Nazis rhetoric his dad spewed out around the house about other races being inferior academically - now Jordan was tearing down those walls of ignorance. As a result, Harry and Jordan formed a "natural bond", free of corrupt bias and could be seen frequently hanging out together at school and they even started walking home from school together. This newfound relationship made Harry Sr. furious.

While the two high school teammates started to form this unlikely bond, Harry Sr. burned with rage. The two-boy's relationship caused an already tension filled household to become extremely volatile. Upon seeing Harry Jr. and Jordan James arrive home together for the first time, Harry met his son at the door in a profanity filled frenzy. Harry proceeded to berate his son. "You're a traitor to your own race, a traitor to America!" Harry Sr shouted in anger. "I don't ever want to see you walking down the street with his kind again!"

This went on for an anxiety filled ten minutes as Harry displayed the behavior of a man out of control. His wife Judy simply stood in the background as she normally did, stunned by the behavior of her husband.

Harry Jr. for his part remained calm, composed as if he were sizing up his father. Finally, Harry Jr. said to his father, "Dad you were wrong about the people across the street and wrong about labeling people simply because they don't look like you. I've gotten to know Jordan and he's one of the best dudes I know and he's also one of the smartest. Jordan is not my enemy." Harry Jr. said and left quietly.

Harry Sr was now being controlled by his hate and white supremacist teachings. He quickly became one of the top online recruiters, writers, and teachers for the group. His high-level technological skills quickly became a huge asset for their organization just as Rex figured they would be when he recruited Harry. Harry went by the pseudonym "Blood & Soil" while online to hide his identity and to maintain his "proper standing" in the community.

Rex, somehow found out about the relationship between Harry's son and the "nigger across the street" he called him. Do you want us to take care of this for you Harry? Rex said. It'll be just like in the good ole days Rex laughed. Nah, I'm going to handle it myself in house, so my son won't suspect anything Harry replied.

Chapter 14

Choices, remembering who you are

Conrad and Jordan sat quietly in the living room. Son, I'm concerned about this new relationship you and Harry Jr. appear to be forming Conrad said. Concerned? why Dad? You have always told me I can do or be anything I wanted, not to limit my relationships to certain groups of people, and no one is above or below me. Jordan stated.

Remember how you told me how Grandma would say we should strive to be different? To live a life that breaks the molds of stereotypes and the categorizing of people? Jordan said.

And I meant it Jordan, it's just this time there could be danger because of the racial component and I don't won't you to get mixed up in it. We've heard some things about his father I have yet to be able to verify, but if it turns out to be true there will be ramifications that come with them and I don't won't you to get hurt is all. Your mom and I just want you to be careful son. Sometimes choosing to hang around the wrong people can get you in trouble Conrad said.

I'll be fine Dad. We'll be fine. I just wish all this old history of racial stuff, and old racist would just die off and allow the new age to come together Jordan said.

That's the problem son those old guard racists are attempting to attract and recruit a new generation of young people. It's why they're so prevalent on the internet. They want to poison the minds of young people with the disease of hate before they die off.

Son, the KKK used to boldly place recruitment ads in local

newspapers but now groups like them are more covert, secret, hiding online behind aliases.

One method they use to identify themselves to one another online is through symbols and numbers. Conrad said. Like 1418 or 1488. The 14 is shorthand for the 14-word Nazi slogan "we must secure the existence of our people and a future for white children". While the 88 is Nazi code for the 8th letter of the alphabet H, is code for Heil Hitler.

As they attempt to become more and more stealth and high-tech, we must combat them in the technological realm as well. They want to leave a legacy of hate not love, divisions not unity. Some of them have got one foot in the grave already, yet they refuse to change.

They're going to leave this earth and stand before God with hate in their hearts. It's a shame Conrad said shaking his head.

Sun Park High School boy's football team went on to win the Texas State football championship. The school campus was in a frenzy with celebrations. The entire campus and community was covered in the bright orange and blue colors of the school.

State dignitaries including the governor came to the Sun Park community for a parade and donations started to pour in from across the state which made the school's principal Frank Watters extremely happy. Mr. Watters declared the school would hold a rally all week for the new state champions as they celebrated their team.

The teams two top stars, Harry Jacobs Jr. and Jordan James became the toast of the town. They were featured in the local newspapers together and traveled throughout the community to various public appearances. They overcame a lot of adversity in the beginning of the school year but showed their true character and bonded together for the good of the team and were now reaping the benefits.

Their actions brought unity to the team at a time when it needed it most and this propelled them to the state title and now the entire town was in a state of delirious excitement. However suddenly, while in the middle of the school's week of celebrations, tragic news struck the tight knit community. Word was starting to get around that one of the team's star players was gravely ill and needed to be rushed to the hospital. The news stunned the small community, putting the entire city into a unified daze and bringing the celebrations to an abrupt halt.

Chapter 15

Confronted by a Choice

Harry Jacobs Jr. lay in a bed at Houston General hospital after collapsing, falling ill upon returning home from one of the many community celebrations being held for the team since its recent state championship. His father and mother followed the ambulance to the hospital and were now impatiently awaiting word on the status of their son.

Cancer! Leukemia! Harry Jacobs Sr. shouted, his voice breaking through the silence of the waiting room as he repeated what Dr. Ruth McKenzie had quietly informed him and his wife. How can that be Harry asked? He's only 17 years old and in great shape. He's one of the top high school football players in the state for crying out loud! Harry said in disbelief as his wife cried in the background.

I know this is difficult news to receive Mr. Jacobs Dr. McKenzie replied. But we've run all the necessary test and we have checked and rechecked our findings and are certain of the results. Your son has what is commonly known as CML (Chronic Myeloid Leukemia) and I'm amazed he could compete in sports and do the things he's been able to do recently.

I'm here now to give you the best options for treatment going forward she said. Unfortunately, your son Harry is at the accelerated phase of the disease and badly in need of a bone marrow transplant. I think we need to start searching the donor registry at bethematch.org immediately for a donor match Dr. McKenzie continued. Normally we would have the option of chemotherapy either with or without radiation first and then try TKI's (tyrosine kinase inhibitors) medicines but since he's in the accelerated stage, I think we ought to go to bethematch.org immediately and look for a match to save his life.

Harry Sr. and Judy sat down in stunned silence as they attempted to absorb this life altering news. After a few minutes Judy looked up at Dr. McKenzie and asked can I be the donor? Me or his father? We can start testing right away to see if either of you are a match. Dr. McKenzie replied.

Are you registered on the bone marrow registry? Are there any other siblings we can test because there is usually a 25% chance for a complete match with a brother or sister. No, he's an only child replied Judy. Unfortunately, about 70% of patients who need a bone marrow donor don't have a close match in their family. If we don't match him with you or Harry Sr. I'll start searching the bethematch.org registry for a match right away.

"One day I hope that everyone would make the choice to register on bethematch.org. We never know when we can save a life or who's." Dr. McKenzie said.

The news of Harry Jacobs Jr.'s illness and need for a bone marrow transplant spread quickly across the Sun Park community. It became headline news and the donor registry in the Houston area increased dramatically as people looked to help however they could. In fact, the entire Sun Park high school football team got together and started their own bone marrow registry drive on the campus and signed up themselves, their classmates as well as several staff members at the school. It seemed the entire community came together to save the life of Harry Jr.

Just when Harry Jr's situation appeared lost, during a time of heartache within the Sun Park community came a ray of hope. There were two individuals who ranked high on the registry as potential matches for Harry Jr. Both lived near the Sun Park community. Dr. McKenzie enthusiastically called the Jacobs home to inform them of the new development. Telling the Jacobs, it was the donors high ranking on the list that makes them a potential match for Harry Jr.

The news gave hope to both Harry and Judy Jacobs who were spiraling downward in emotional turmoil, infusing a much-needed dose of optimism into a dejected household.

"Our son can still be saved after all!" shouted the normally reserved Judy bringing a tear to the eye of Harry Sr.

I knew God would not let us down Harry replied. Rex has been teaching in the meetings how God has a special place in his heart for white people. This is confirmation of it Harry continued.

Dr. McKenzie then followed up with the two men from the bethematch.org registry who appeared to be potential matches. She eagerly waited for them to come in for the needed testing to move them into the next phase of bone marrow donation. However, she stressed to them the timing was critical as the potential patient was in the accelerated phase of his leukemia, so she was eager to get started.

Dr. McKenzie was only able to speak directly with one of the two potential matches. The other she was forced to leave multiple phone and email messages for and was still awaiting a response. It both frustrated and puzzled her how someone who took the time to sign up for this life saving registry could procrastinate in response to this urgent call.

Jordan James received the surprise call from the hospital and now found himself in a position he or his family could have never envisioned a few months earlier. Jordan could possibly be the key to saving the life of his friend and teammate Harry Jr. He was once considered an adversary or possibly even an enemy. A person who hated Jordan simply because of the color of his skin.

Harry was taught to believe things about his people that were not only false but done out of hatred and malice. Masking the true purpose of these erroneous teachings which was giving themselves political, social, and economic advantages. Jordan shook his head at the irony of the situation. The thought of having the conversation with his parents about what he may have to do made him nervous.

When Harry Sr. was made aware that Jordan James was one of the two potential bone marrow donors his mood changed from one of optimism to gloom. To Harry Sr. this was a great dilemma he now found his family in. Rex was currently teaching them on the importance of preserving the "pure white blood." "We have a duty to God and country to preserver pure white blood. To defend our heritage and way of life" Rex said to Harry during one of his sessions. "This is how we are able to remain superior to the Jews, blacks, and Hispanics. It's our pure white blood that makes us genetically superior, more intelligent."

That's right God made us more intelligent! It's God's will for the "master race" to preserves its blood. This may sound cruel Harry Rex said, but how else are we going to take care of those inferior races? He asked. It's a part of God's plan.

Those niggers, and spics would be lost without us. They are like animals who need care from us. And don't be fooled by the Jews skin color either. They are our enemies as well. Their goal is to replace us, and they need to be annihilated just as Adolf Hitler intended to do. One day we are going to finish what Hitler started. The words of Rex which sounded so profound before, now echoed in the head of Harry Sr.

upon learning the bone marrow/blood transfusion match was Jordan James.

This news sent both the James and Jacobs households located directly across the street from each on a seesaw of emotions. Jordan notified his parents and they were meeting with him about the situation. I don't know son I know you want to help your teammate out but this is a major step.

It wasn't long ago when the Jacobs family wanted to run us off the block. His father still does Conrad said. Janice stepped in saying Yeah, but I can tell he wants to do it. He wants to save his friends life. You've come a long way baby and I'm proud of the progress you and Harry Jr. have made.

I remember when you told us he was a racist and back then you seemed to despise one another Janice continued. He's changed mom! Replied Jordan to both. He became a different person right before my eyes. We became the two closest guys on the team Said Jordan. I Just want you to be careful around those people, the friends his father hangs out with.

The things they are teaching one another are dangerous. Conrad said. I understand pop Said Jordan. I wish you and his father could have gotten to know one another the way we have, maybe things would be different between you two as well. Jordan said.

Maybe son, maybe in a different life. You're 18 years old and we're not going to stand in your way, but I have my reservations said Conrad. We'll support you whatever you decide.

Meanwhile, Harry Sr. and Judy Jacobs were engaged in a heated argument and the normally submissive and reserved Judy Jacobs could be heard screaming at a deafening level.

The couple went back and forth about options before them. To Judy there were no options. Our son has been given a second chance at life, God has provided an answer to our prayers.

You would choose to remain stuck in your own hate at the risk of losing our son? Judy said emphatically. Harry was adamant; God would never be behind the mixing of "pure white blood" with the "blood of a nigger". That's the crap you and that group you belong to have been getting people riled up about which has nothing to do with God Judy said. It has everything to do with God! Said Harry and stormed out of the house to meet with his fellow white supremacist group members.

Chapter 16

Choices that Reveal the Condition of the Heart

Harry Jacobs Sr arrived at the meeting with white his fellow white supremacist filled with anger. After storming out of the house following the fight with his wife. Discovering one of the matches that could potentially save his son's life came from Jordan James was hard for Harry to accept. "No way I'm allowing nigger blood to taint our family blood lines." Harry said as he pulled into the driveway.

Upon entering, Rex and the others in the group of about 25 white men could immediately sense the anger emanating from him. They all knew about the crisis facing the Jacobs family with the extreme condition of Harry Jr. however, they were also excited because Harry updated them with the news of two potential matches for the bone marrow transplant. The men were eager to greet Harry expecting him to be in a cheerful mood but Harry's demeanor changed the tone of their greeting.

Harry explained to his "white brethren" that the young black neighbor across the street was one of the matches, and they have yet to hear back from the other possible match. They were all in unison, preaching the preservation of the "pure white blood" and the white race.

How can a nigger be a match for pure white blood? Shouted one member. This is outrageous, no way a nigger can give a blood transfusion to a pure white man! Shouted another. It must be another trick of the Jews! One was heard screaming. You sure the Doctor is not a Jew? You have to be careful they try to pass themselves off as white sometimes.

What about the second donor do you know who it is yet? someone shouted to Harry. I don't know Harry responded. But if he has the same blood as that monkey then what's the difference. He couldn't possibly be one of our people even if his skin is white! said Harry slamming his fist on the table in front of him.

Rex sat there in silent amazement at the news of the black kid across the street was a compatible and comparable match for the same person as he was. He was planning to surprise Harry at the meeting tonight by informing him he was the other match the hospital was attempting to reach. Rex was intending to go there in the morning for the needed test but hearing the men he referred to as his "white brethren" and their responses to the news about a "nigger" giving the blood transfusion to the son of one of the "white brethren" made him rethink what he was going to do.

Rex now had his own choice to make as his mind raced over the options before him. Should I save the life of my brother's son and risk being exposed as having the same blood as a black kid? Rex, who was the founder and leader of this Neo Nazi sect thought to himself, "I can't allow this information to get out. It would hurt the movement."

I may be able to save the life of Harry's son but at what cost? Dr. McKenzie said the timing was critical and Harry Jr. was in the accelerated stage when she left me the message. However, if anyone believed a "pure white Christian man like me" had the same blood as a jungle monkey, it could cause long-term damage to our cause and to the white race.

Rex finally spoke up to the group of his brothers and to

Harry specifically. Brother Harry, I know it has been a hard week for you and it may seem dark right now but take heart, the "white Christian God" will send you the answer and he would not send you one that would taint the "pure white blood."

Our brothers speak the truth when they say you can't taint the "pure white blood" with a blood transfusion from one of those people. Our bothers all over the world would disown you, he would no longer be white but a mixed race, an outcast like those Samaritans in the bible.

Rex decided at that moment he would choose his own personal agenda over the life of the son of his "white brethren".

But he wanted to go even further by stopping one of the men in his local sect from submitting to something he thought could make them look bad nationally. Rex hoped to one day become the national leader of the Neo Nazis group. He now believed Harry Sr. allowing the bone marrow of the black kid to be transplanted in his son would make him look bad and derail his chances of becoming the national leader.

Harry went home that night determined to change his wife's mind about allowing Jordan to be the bone marrow donor. He had developed a trust in Rex who took advantage of the past failures in his life. Failures which still haunted him even to this day. Especially the rejection he believed that came from his father not accepting him for the person he was.

The weight of these emotions caused Harry to carry a "spirit of rejection" around with him. The burden of it was used by Rex to nurture hatred for others. Rex, it seemed filled the void Harry felt in his heart from his father's rejection of him; and the white supremacist members the hole of him not making the team in school.

It was the level of trust Rex developed in Harry which allowed him to believe any words Rex told him. "The white Christian God will send you the answer, and he would not send you one that would taint the pure white blood."

later the same evening in the middle of the night at the home of Conrad and Janice James. The family was already gone to bed for the night when they heard a knock on their bedroom door. Jordan is that you? Why are you up so late tonight son? Janice called out to her son.

Jordan pierced through the dark bedroom of his mother and father, breaking through the still quiet of the night. Tears welling up in his eyes with the look of someone unable to sleep, instead consumed by his thoughts.

"I want to do it!" Jordan said firmly to his parents. His emotions getting the best of him as he started to cry, his voice cracking as he spoke. Dad, you've always told me grandma would say we should always strive to be different. To live a life that breaks free from the stereotypes and categorizing of people and not allow anyone to limit me in any way Jordan said. All true son said Conrad about to continue, but Jordan jumped back in. Grandma always told me to always chose right over wrong, and love over hate.

She'd say to never give up on doing good. It's what the "good book" told her she would always say. "Grandma would want me to do it. I don't care if his family members hate me or how they feel about black people, immigrants or anything, that's what I want to do!"

It was an emotional and defining moment in the James home as both parents got up to hug their son. Emotions poured out of the three of them bringing their entire family to tears. They lay there together in bed for the next hour. I'm so proud of you son. Conrad said to Jordan. I know you've accomplished a lot in school and on the football field, but this decision is far greater than any of those things Conrad said as he wiped a tear from his face. Tomorrow we'll go with you to the hospital to get things moving in the right direction so you can help your friend. I know you're concerned about him and his condition requires immediate action.

Dr. McKenzie said the timing is critical, and he's badly in need of the bone marrow. She said it was a matter of life and death.

Harry Sr arrived home that evening a man with a purpose and mission. Emboldened by the words of support from the men he called his "white brethren" now determined to not allow the bone marrow donation from Jordan James. His goal now was to convince his wife this was the best thing to do for their son despite the urgency of the moment. His wife Judy met him at the door to inquire about how long he'd been away from the house in their time of need.

Judy Jacobs only concern now was saving the life of their only son Harry Jr. She knew about Harry Sr. participating in the white supremacy group but never spoke out against it. She remained silent and complicit as the teachings of the sect transformed her husband into the hate filled man he currently was. Now she wanted to speak up to have him defy the group's leadership and save their sons life.

Harry was already armed with the teachings of the Nazis doctrine and ready to combat her resistance. He told her the "white Christian God" would send them the solution and heal their son of his leukemia and bone cancer! The "white Christian God" would never provide a solution involving the mixing of pure white blood with the blood of a nigger. God wants us to preserve the pure white race! God has a special place in his heart for white people! All we have to do is keep praying and God will provide us with an acceptable answer. Harry told his wife.

Remember there is a second donor out there who Dr. McKenzie has been reaching out to, and I'll bet he's a white man Harry said. In the end, the submissive Judy Jacobs gave in to her husband's request and trusted he knew and would choose what was best for them and their family.

Chapter 17

We get to Choose the path that we travel in life

Two months into the school year at Sun Park High and not a lot had changed for Oliver Jones and Henry Allen. The bullying, although not happening as much on the school property after Howard Fletcher Sr. spoke with his son and his group of friends intensified via online and all types of electronic media. Oliver and Henry both seemingly walked around the school with a bullseye on their backs. Feeling dejected, having no friends, and ostracized from all other relationships but the one they shared together. Their misery became their common bond.

For many of the students on the Sun Park campus, attempting to fit in with some of the "popular kids" was their priority. For others, it was fear they also would become targets of harassment. The fear prevented them from stepping up, speaking up and bringing an end to the relentless bullying. Instead they formed their own group of silence to avoid retaliation from other students for daring to speak in the face of this harsh treatment of Oliver and Henry.

The administration was in its fundraising season and did not want to allow any negative news to seep out about the school causing them to be unresponsive and unwilling to challenge their largest benefactor Mr. Howard Fletcher, the person most responsible for the funding for the expansive Howard Fletcher Technology Center which now was the centerpiece of the campus. This systematic silence from the administration trickled down to the staff and other students making the situation appear hopeless and intolerable to

Oliver and Henry.

Howard Fletcher Jr. still led his online bullying group. A member suggested, instead of wasting the $5,000 bounty on those "two geeks", let's have the biggest party of the year and we can come together and blast them on social media at the same time.

In fact, that could be the theme of the party. We can call it as an "anti-geek party" that should get us a lot of attention from the other students and we'll really let them have it that day. We can go down in history as the greatest ever.

They laughed themselves to exhaustion at the thought of how much fun they would have at the expense of Oliver and Henry.

Oliver and Henry had gotten to the point where they geared themselves up mentally to make it through most school days. However, as the days grew more unbearable, they came up with new and creative ways to not attend. Some days they would fake an illness or sickness, others they would invent field trips or school outings, while some days they simply pretended to go and ditched school.

The boys had become experts at inventing creative ways to skip school. The cyberbullying they were experiencing dissipated for a moment during the week of distractions, but with things slowing down the tormenting appeared to be reenergized. Mistreatment became the "new normal" for Oliver and Henry, and for the students who bullied them as well. The two-year period of harassment already isolated and ostracized the two teens from all the other students on the Sun Pak campus. Although stigmatized as outcast by the ordeal, they were brought even closer together by their shared pain.

It was the pain, despair, and hopelessness pulling at them, driving them to the brink of lashing out and being tempted to act on the anger bubbling inside of them and giving in to the cruelty of people by ending their own lives. Henry who previously suffered from the mental illness of depression was now being challenged to maintain his mental stability. This time his best friend Oliver Jones promised him if he needed to return to receive more counseling, he would attend along with him.

Just when it appeared the oppression could get no worse for Oliver and Henry the tone took a dark turn. The bullying group's cruel jokes turned to the possibility of suicide. First came this via social media to them "suicide is the second leading cause of death among teenagers can you help us make it number one:) :)" read the first. "Kill yourselves" someone followed. "Why are you still alive" came next.

"What could be better than a suicide pact between friends:)" someone texted. Death is better than life for some people. Hahahaha! I'll bet you two are too cowardly to kill yourselves! Nobody likes you it would be easier to die:). On and on this went as one person followed the next attempting to outdo the last in their level of cruelty.

Howard Fletcher Jr. the leader of the group along with his circle of friends planned the "anti-geek party" for the weekend. They were fervidly promoting it at school and online. Thanks to the $5,000 raised for their terrorizing prank at the start of the school year. Believing this party could be something more memorable, crueler, more hurtful.

An event they could relive over and over while generating a huge following on social media. People could participate in person as well as online live or some other type of media. There would be drinking, dancing, partying, however the main course would be the bullying. Everything was set and ready for their big day.

On Saturday morning, the day of the party Oliver came to visit Henry. They both had gotten their parent's permission for a sleepover by falsely claiming to have a science project to work on. Oliver was shocked by what he saw when he entered his friend's bedroom. Wow! Where did you get all of these guns Henry? Oliver asked in amazement. I am taking up a new hobby said Henry. I think I want to take up target shooting, I'm told it can be very relaxing and I need to relieve some stress. Me and you both. Oliver said.

But how were you able to buy a gun with your mental health record? I didn't think you could buy a gun if you've been treated for depression or any type of mental illness. Did you buy these guns on the street or something? Oliver asked. No man I went into a regular gun store and bought one. I just showed the man my id to prove I was 18years old and that's all he cared about. They don't care if you're a serial killer man, we'll sell a gun to anyone who wants one in America Henry said while laughing.

The man at the gun store also gave me a tip about gun shows. There you can buy as many guns and ammo as you'd like with no background check or anything. It's where I got the arsenal of semi-automatic rifles, military style guns, and all this ammunition.

It was easier than buying cough medicine. You have to be 21 years old to do that but only 18 to buy all these guns. They sell guns like candy at a gun show laughed Henry.

Later that same night there was a new onslaught of texts, social media posts, emails directed at both Oliver and Henry. They were coming in by the hundreds at a time. A flurry of activity coming so fast and furious the messages were almost unreadable. The velocity and speed of the incoming messages was surpassed only by the level of cruelty exhibited by the senders. The two boys were accustomed to receiving large volumes of vicious messages, but something about this time was different.

The avalanche of messages coming in from all types of media overwhelmed them, engulfed them, rocked them to their core. How come so many people hate us? Henry asked with desperation in his voice. They don't even know us replied Oliver. These people are just wicked and evil. It's like something about being on the internet and having an electronic device that make people lose their minds or become possessed.

Howard Fletcher and his group were at the party having a "great time" at the expense of Oliver and Henry. They were also hosting it online and invited people from all over to actively participate with them in their game of ruthlessness. With each succeeding message the level of inhumanity sank lower and lower as people attempted to one up each other. In one night, the boys received over 20,000 messages from all over the world.

They sat in stunned silence. I think we ought to do it Oliver Henry said. Do what? replied Oliver. Kill ourselves, at least then the pain will be over, and we can do it together and not die alone. This loneliness is unbearable at times said Henry. Or we can we strike back! Oliver said defiantly. Instead of us being victims, if we are going to die, I say we take as many of them bastards with us as possible. What do you mean? Henry asked. I mean on Monday morning we walk into the school and get our revenge for the last two years of hell they've put us through. For all the insults, the tormenting, the embarrassing name calling, all of it! We have all the weapons and guns we need for war!

Let's make out our hitlist tonight so when we go to school on Monday morning, we'll know who our main targets are Oliver said, already having the name Howard Fletcher etched in his mind.

It's time to make them pay Henry, every one of them bastards must pay! Oliver said with determination. But wouldn't that make us as bad as them Oliver? Henry asked. It was their choice to be bullies! It's time for them to learn that choices have consequences! If we don't stop them, soon they'll be hounding someone else! Besides I'm tired of being the victim. It's time to take back our power! "We get to choose the path that we travel in life" Said Oliver.

Chapter 18

Choices affect those closest to you

Andre Jackson sat quietly in stark contrast to everyone else inside of the large banquet hall for employees, family, and friends of WKROC TV news. Andre felt nervous, anxious, and uneasy. His aura contradicted the mood of the room as he sat alone in the crowd of people there to celebrate.

Word was out the WKROC would be given an award for the highest rated news station of the year. The atmosphere was bubbling with excitement, however Andre remained alone at his table as he waited for his wife Daphne and their daughter Renae to arrive.

Wanting to share this moment with them rendered him unable to give-in to the elation of the moment. He talked with his wife Daphne throughout the year and listened to her concerns about some of the choices he was making for the station's direction.

As he reflected on some of those decisions he believed tonight would be the crowning moment when he looked back on those choices and saw it had all been worth it.

He recalled what Paul told him earlier in the day, that he would be winning the award for the top news executive of the year, but he was thinking "bigger picture". He was ready to be in a position of influence and change in the news media industry. "I want to promote fair and equal treatment of all people in media" Andre thought to himself.

Andre realized he and Paul were capitalizing on old systematic stereotyping based on race and now with the national focus on immigration and the passions exhibited by both sides of the issue it was easy to portray false or misleading narratives and generate higher ratings. Andre had convinced himself that his short-term choices to sacrifice his own personal integrity, beliefs, and even his dignity at times would lead to a position of importance where in the long-term he could help create systematic change in the media industry.

Andre hoped Paul would be correct. Once they both were recognized as top executives in the news media industry, they would then have the power to create systematic change. "Oh! Do I need for Paul to be right!" Andre said to himself.

The most important moment of my career and she's running late Andre thought to himself looking around as the awards ceremony began. He became increasingly agitated, wondering what was taking his wife Daphne so long to arrive. Several awards were announced and the large crowd in attendance was getting more and more enthusiastic with each winner. Soon it would be time for the announcements of the two most coveted awards in the industry. News Station of the Year. Followed by News Executive of the Year.

The program called for a 15-minute break now and people were moving about in a festive mood. In the next room for WKROC TV everything was setup for the party which would be taking place immediately following the awards banquet.

The entire room now seemed to be on their telephones, some calling, others on social media, taking pictures, or broadcasting themselves live. Andre started feverishly making calls to Daphne. His initial agitation with the tardiness of his wife had evolved into worry, and now was approaching the panic stage.

Andre was unable to reach Daphne despite spending the entire break dialing her phone over and over again. Andre cussed in frustration! His mind raced from one potential reason for his wife's absence to another. Could she have changed her mind about attending? No, he said to himself. Although Daphne didn't agree with what they were doing at the station, she would never miss the biggest night of his career. This thought caused him to worry even more. The music started playing in the background as it was time to recommence with the awards.

The emcee was back at the podium making the final two presentations which were the most coveted awards of the night. The winner of the station of the year awarded to the station with the highest ratings goes to WKROC TV in Sun Park, TX.

The announcement was followed by thunderous applause and loud shouts. Andre sat silently, stoic, a picture of contrast to the surroundings he sat in the middle of. Now down to the last award of the night and the crowd of people in attendance were giddy with anticipation. Andre looked around one final time for Daphne and Renae to come through the door; now completely numb to the proceedings.

"The winner of the award for News Executive of the year goes to Andre Jackson from WKROC TV news in Houston". Andre slowly walked to the podium to accept his "coveted" award. The accolade he believed would make all the difference in his life. This was the award that was going to put him into a "position of power and influence" he told himself. Make him a power broker in the news media industry in SE Texas.

Andre was receiving a standing ovation by the time he reached the podium. Glancing up again to check for his wife he felt an emptiness on the inside. "Something is wrong." Andre said to himself. The lack of fulfillment he felt from receiving something he worked so hard to obtain created an emptiness inside of him.

Andre pulled out some prepared remarks from the inside of his jacket. Just as he started to speak there was a huge commotion at the door. Everyone in the room turned their attention towards the noise as four police officers entered the room asking questions from those in attendance. The people they talked to were pointing at Andre and the officers then diverted their attention to him. They started making their way in his direction. Andre came down off the platform to meet them. He and the officers met in the middle of the room and huddled together for a short time as the crowd looked on in bewilderment.

Andre Jackson then collapsed into the arms of one of the officers. The crowd of onlookers gasped in horror at the sight of seeing the hero of the night, the person they were attempting to honor struck down by the news relayed to him by the policemen. Andre Jackson was rushed to Houston General hospital with the belief his wife and daughter were killed by a burglar soon after he left home.

People who were standing nearby overheard the policemen tell Andre about the break-in at his home and the murder of his wife and daughter. Word started to flow through the audience like streams of flowing water. Loud screams of sorrow erupted from the crowd. Some became distraught and could be heard sobbing loudly and uncontrollably. Still others seemed almost paralyzed, frozen in disbelief at the tragic news striking one of their own. The night of celebration was turned into a night wailing.

Chapter 19

Wrong Choices come with Unintended Consequences

By the time Andre arrived at Houston General Hospital his mind was blank, and bare of thoughts. Police officer Eric Kemp who drove Andre to the hospital questioned him about anything he may have seen, his activities of the night leading up to his wife's murder, but Andre never responded to any of the questions.

Andre literally never heard a word the officer said to him as he stared out of the window of the squad car in a daze. His mind numb to his surroundings; hiding the pain he was feeling. It became a temporary shield against the night's crisis, an escape from the reality of the moment. A coping mechanism from the brain to provide the heart with temporary relief from the agony. He was hoping it was a dream, but the pain felt real.

Noticing that Andre was not moving as they sat parked in front of the hospital entrance in an awkward moment of silence, Police Officer Eric Kemp turned to Andre. We're here he said in an official tone, jarring Andre from his trance, and asking if it would be ok if he walked him inside of the building. There he would attempt to get some information from him about his wife and daughter.

Once inside Andre seemed to snap to himself for a moment. Officer Kemp questioned him for some routine information about his wife. Already pronounced dead at their home. Which was now a crime scene. Officer Kemp hoped to also get an update on the condition of his daughter Renae. She appeared to be near death last he saw her but was not yet pronounced to be. He looked at Andre with compassion and couldn't help what came out of his mouth next.

"This is such a tragedy; we were standing right in front of this guy! The suspect Avery Wright not more than 30 minutes prior to him breaking into your house. He was wanted for several home invasions in the area when a news report came over the TV.

At the time, we were less than three feet from him but the vague description that came over the news channel was useless. By the time I could obtain a more accurate and detailed description of the suspect he was gone.

"I don't understand, we gave those news stations detailed descriptions of the suspect to use. If not for them, this tragedy could have been avoided!" Said Officer Kemp shaking his head.

Officer Kemp was caught up in the emotion of the situation and blurted out those details in frustration as he sat beside Andre, unaware Andre himself played a huge roll in WKROC's TV news plan to exploit racial bias for higher ratings. Why would they do something like that? Officer Kemp repeated almost to himself.

What station was it? Andre replied in a whisper like tone fearing he already knew the answer. Not sure something with ROC or something in the title replied the officer as he walked off to speak to the nurse.

With this additional information from Officer Kemp, Andre sank down in his seat and back into the temporary escape from reality his mind provided him. Not long after he started to revisit some of the decisions he made, the poor choices that led to this dreadful calamity. The choice to go against his own principles and standards of right and wrong.

Was it for the long term good of the industry like I sold myself on? Was I trying to make a difference in my community? No! It all sounded noble and good at the time, but this was done for personal recognition and career gain he concluded in a moment of honest reflection.

Two quotes he couldn't stop thinking about resonated like clapping thunder going off in his head. The first was his wife Daphne's "You don't need a position to have influence." The other one was from his news anchor Pricilla Prescott, in objection to exploiting racial division and stereotypes "Just remember Andre, we're all only one person away from knowing someone who has been victimized by the senseless gun violence going on in our country." Andre cussed to himself out of frustration. These things combined with Officer Kemp's new information about the suspect pushed Andre into a state of despair.

Andre was sinking lower and lower into gloom and darkness as the moment overwhelmed him. The entire room appeared to be spiraling down as the emotions emanating from Andre filled the atmosphere. Under the grip of anguish, Andre said to himself "this is all my fault" as tears streamed down his face. But suddenly, came a ray of hope as Dr. McKenzie emerged from surgery to speak with Andre. She was one of the few surgeons in the world equipped to handle the surgery for Renae because of how close the bullet came to piercing her heart.

Walking with purpose, and at a brisk pace she approached Andre who was slumped down in his seat in the waiting room. Mr. Jackson I'm Dr. McKenzie and I came to update you on your daughter's condition. She said. Andre never moved other than glancing up at the doctor believing Renae was already dead; he attempted to brace himself for the news. We did remove the bullet which was only centimeters away from her heart, and it looks like she's going to make it. Her condition is critical, but stable, but I'm optimistic about her chances.

Andre's face lit up as her words gave him the needed strength to stand to his feet. Hearing the news that his daughter was still alive drastically changed his emotions, shifting them from despair to joy, hopelessness to elation. Andre was overcome with emotions as he cried uncontrollably, falling into the arms of the doctor.

Dr. McKenzie was scheduled for a long overdue vacation, but she decided to reschedule it as she was the doctor working on Harry Jacobs Jr. Still in grave condition due to his unforeseen leukemia diagnosis, and badly in need of a bone marrow transplant. A gift that would breathe life into a dead situation for Andre and his daughter.

Chapter 20

The right Choice over the easy Choice

The next morning Dr. McKenzie was making her rounds and came back to check on Andre who was still in the hospital waiting room hoping to see Renae when she came out of her sleep. Dr. McKenzie had completed her shift, however she invited him to walk with her to have coffee in the cafeteria of the hospital. What was intended to be a brief meeting between them turned into a one-hour conversation/counseling session as they discussed both personal and professional topics.

Seeing Andre was now recovered sufficiently, Dr. McKenzie then made a professional recommendation to him. I think you should meet with someone here at the hospital the doctor suggested. He has helped a lot of people get through similar situations She said.

Situations like what? replied Andre.

Dealing with grief. In fact, he is the grief counsellor here and an expert in the field replied Dr. McKenzie.

Andre attempted to ignore the issue, wanting to remain enveloped in his cocoon of pain to punish himself for the poor choices he made. He tried changing the subject. "They tell me you are one of the few doctors on staff here, and in the world who could have performed the surgery on my daughter. I guess we got lucky having you huh?"

Lucky? replied Dr. McKenzie emphatically. I don't believe in luck. I believe in people making good choices, preparing behind the scenes, and God. "luck" happens when preparation and opportunity intersect, then miracles happen!

Dr. McKenzie said convincingly.

I'll share something personal with you Andre. I'm adopted, and before I was even born, my biological mother, who was a teenager at the time, contemplated having an abortion. Apparently, in her inner circle was a deeply religious friend who talked her out of it and recommended she give me up for adoption instead.

Reluctantly, she listened to her friend and carried me the whole nine months; giving me up to a great family for adoption at birth.

They tell me I'm one of the best surgeons in the world Andre. I've been blessed to have the opportunity to impact the lives of hundreds if not thousands of people including your daughter Renae last night. All because of the choice made by a nervous and frightened teenager to save my life. Now, does that sound like luck to you Andre?

Not when you put it like that he said.   He sat there in awe of the revelation from her and thankful Dr. McKenzie was alive to be there for Renae's surgery.

Dr. Louis Hernandez is the name of the grief counselor she continued.   We first met over twenty years ago. It wasn't a formal meeting, we met through life's circumstances caused by the poor choices of one individual. My brother from my adopted family and I were hanging out at the local park one day when a fight broke out on the basketball court.

We had no idea what was going on, nor were we interested in finding out. As we started to leave gun shots rang out between the two groups. My brother was hit by a stray bullet and killed.

Dr. Louis Hernandez was with the person who mindlessly started firing shots and killed my brother. Frankie Alvarez was his name. He and Louis grew up together and were best friends.

We were both still in high school at the time, but Louis and I still talk about that day 20 years ago and it helps us both get through the tough times.

    They both sat in silence contemplating how circumstances neither of them could have foreseen had brought them together. Damn life! Andre said to himself.

Chapter 21

Time sensitive choices

It was the middle of the night at Houston General Hospital, but Harry Jacobs Jr. was awake, lying in his bed contemplating life. He was a 17-year-old five-star athlete; a high school all American quarterback who recently won the Texas state championship for his school. "I should be out having fun, studying, or making my decision about college soon and here I am laying in this bed with barley enough strength to get up and walk" Harry Jr. said to himself in his lonely and darkened room. Harry felt disheartened, sorrowful, but not angry. He was strangely at peace.

Leukemia! Cancer! Wow! I didn't even realize a person my age could get something like that Harry Jr. said. He accomplished a lot in his short life Harry Jr. thought to himself and smiled. He thought about his own transformation from the beginning of the school year until now. I was crazy in the beginning. Harry laughed to himself shaking his head.

He and Jordan James became the best of friends and accomplished a lot together. "I almost allowed my father's racial hatred for others to corrupt me as well." Harry Jr said. I can't spend the rest of my life thinking and feeling like that. Hate is a waste of time, energy, and it hurts the person carrying the hate more than anyone else. Harry said as he thought about his dad and how the self-inflicted burden of hate changed him into a different person over the past year.

Without warning feeling weak again, and about to be overcome by his illness, Harry Jr decided to roll over and go back to sleep. I can't even stay awake for an hour he said and feel asleep.

Waking up again and turning over he saw his cell phone sitting there powered off. Harry Jr. reached for his phone; he'd been isolated from the world since his sickness. "Having Leukemia and being in dire need of a blood transfusion made things like being on social media, number of likes or shares, and friend request seem trivial" Harry Jr said to himself managing a laugh. I think that was my first laugh in about a week he thought.

Opening his phone Harry Jr. was astounded by what he saw; the number of notifications, and messages on his social media accounts were outrageously high. He quickly clicked on a couple of the messages intrigued by what was going on. Oh, no! Said Harry Jr becoming upset at what he was witnessing, someone has got to do something to stop this madness. Although exhausted from the effects of his cancer; with his hands visibly shaking as he struggled to complete a search on his phone Harry Jr. managed to find the phone number for Margaret Jones; the mother of Oliver Jones.

Harry Jr. quickly dialed the phone number without receiving an answer. This he repeated three times getting the same result. He then called out to the nurse for assistance, but she had just left her station to help another patient and was unable to hear Harry's low tone due to his weakened condition. Harry started to look at more of the messages and then went to the pages of both Oliver Jones and Henry Allen; their last post simply read "revenge day"!

Harry said a quick prayer and decided to dial the number of Margaret Jones one last time. Hello this is Margaret. She said. Mrs. Jones my name is Harry Jacobs you don't know me, but I attend Sun Park High School with your son Oliver. Harry said. Of course, I know who you are Harry the whole town is pulling for you. I'm so sorry to hear about your illness. I hope you are feeling better soon. Margaret said. Thank you, Mrs. Jones, but there is something important that I called to speak to you about. It's your son Oliver and his friend Henry.

I've been out of circulation for a few days, but I just found out they are being bullied a lot at school and mercilessly online. I believe something drastic is about to happen. I think you ought to check on them to see if they are doing ok. Harry said. Bullied? How bad is it? And how long has this been going on? Margaret said. It looks like for a while; Oliver must have been keeping this from you; holding it all inside, I guess Harry replied. Thank you for reaching out to me Harry I was just about to leave out for work. I have an extremely important presentation to get to this morning, but I'll check on them first.

Harry Jacobs Jr. then rolled over in his bed; he smiled to himself feeling content, at peace. It was as if he had completed a mission, an assignment with his name on it. Thank you, God. Harry Jr. said aloud.

Now exhausted from the cancer he fell into a deep sleep. Harry Jr. didn't know at the time that his words "Thank you, God" would be the last words he would ever say. And his phone call the last act of his life.

Chapter 22

Decisions during times of Crisis

Margaret Jones had spent the past year attempting to get an appointment with the new head of HEE Inc. Conrad James, who quickly became one of the most influential people in the Houston area. "Stepping out on faith" she started her own advertising company and landed several small accounts already, enough to pay the bills, but nothing earth shattering" she told a friend. Getting an account, the size of HEE would "significantly change my life, and my family." Margaret said.

Margaret had finally gotten the appointment after a lot of hard work, perseverance, and resourcefulness. Today was the day of the appointment. "Monday morning 9am sharp" echoed in her head recalling what the assistant for Conrad told her. "This is the biggest appointment of my life, the most important of my career. I will make this my number one priority over the next couple of days." She declared. I feel like this is almost life or death Margaret said to herself. "My son and I have been barely getting by, but this could change everything."

After receiving the call from Harry Jr. Margaret walked over to her son Oliver's room but missed him. As she looked out of the bedroom window, she could see him and Henry driving off for school. She called Oliver's phone but got no answer then she tried Henry's with the same result.

Strange she said. I know they saw my number coming up. They looked ok from here she convinced herself. Well at least I know they're on the way to school she said. "I have to keep my focus on this appointment. I can't allow anything to distract me at this moment. I'll deal with the boys and the school later. I should be done with the presentation by 10am and I'll head directly to the school then." Margaret assured herself. Giving comfort to her mind and calming her spirit.

As she drove towards her meeting, she started to get nervous because of the importance she placed on the presentation. "The biggest of my career"; "this could be life changing." Girl you can do this! Encouraging herself. You got this! She continued on with her renewed confidence.

Suddenly, she became struck by feelings of fear and anxiety. Her thoughts now horrified her and she became convinced something was terribly wrong. The conversation between her and Harry Jr. played back in her head. "The boys were being bullied at school and mercilessly online." Harry Jr said. They did look kind of weird and it was strange that neither of them answered my calls. She thought. Margaret attempted to continue to the presentation but her mind was instantly gripped by fear again. It started to build, becoming stronger with each passing second.

She pulled the car over for a moment attempting to calm herself. What is wrong with me? She thought taking a deep breath. Margaret instinctively called Oliver again with no answer. I can't wait to get this appointment over with she said and started driving again. Without warning a sense of pending doom came over her. The fear was back! This time even stronger. It now evolved into horror, panic, an ominous feeling of pending doom. "Oliver! Henry! No! she said to herself. "This can't wait I must act now something bad is about to happen I can feel it!"

Making an illegal U-turn in the middle of traffic she sped towards the school.   Other drivers honked their horns loudly at her reckless maneuver.

She called the office of Conrad James and cancelled the "most important appointment of my life" and raced towards Sun Park High School.

Something was pulling her, telling her the kids were in great trouble. Was it a sixth sense? Women's intuition? Whatever it was she could no longer ignore it. Call it a mother's love. Although she wanted badly to meet with Conrad James and his team and obtain a "life changing account", her conscience got the best of her and she choose to cancel the meeting and take immediate action to save her son.

Now with her heart pounding and in a race against time she was zooming in the opposite direction of her "appointment of a lifetime", heading towards her true destiny - her son.

Arriving at the school just prior to the start of classes she could see the students hanging out, socializing, and getting in last minute conversations. She did not see Oliver and Henry so she tried them one last time on their cell phones with no answer.

Her eyes darted quickly across the landscape, hoping to spot them. With her mind frenzied and heart overwrought with emotions she attempted to calm herself again. Then she remembered where she would drop them off at times. There was a secluded area in the back of the school. The boys would have her use as a drop-off point saying they didn't want to be seen having their mother dropping them off.

When she pulled around back, she could see them. Exiting the car, she sprinted towards them, breathing heavily, but running on adrenaline. When Oliver and Henry saw her, they stopped in their tracks. Mom what are you doing here? Oliver said. I came to see about you and Henry, I've been getting crazy feelings all morning that something was terribly wrong and you boys needed my help. Margaret said.

I also got a call from Harry Jr. the football star here and he said you guys have been getting bullied badly. Not anymore, today is our revenge day Mrs. Jones said Henry. Today we take back our power. They both pulled out their weapons to show them to her. Two AK-47 assault rifles along with semi-automatic pistols.

Margaret Jones was horrified by the revelation. I'm not going to let you two throw your lives away and hurt innocent people while doing it she said. But mom we're tired of the constant bullying, the constant harassment. We're not going to hurt everyone we have a "hit list" prepared.

It's time for us to put an end to all of this even if we must pay with our own lives said Oliver. Your lives are just beginning and they are not required as payment. I am not about to allow you to give in to those types of evil thoughts, I love both of you too much and I promise we'll put an end to all this madness the right way without paying such a high price Margaret said. She grabbed the boys in a bear hug, and they all fell to the ground weeping and releasing the weapons.

Margaret's decisive actions, not ignoring the promptings of her inner spirit, and making the right choice; averted a tragedy on the Sun Park campus that day. She then phoned the Sun Park police department to come up to the school to retrieve the guns. They also took the two boys into custody.

Her next call was to the school's principle to inform him of what happened. And to demand answers from the administration as to why this has been allowed to go on at the school without her knowledge and for so long.

She had questions… "was there any documentation of the previous complaints about bullying at this school?" "What procedures have you put in place to deal with the problem of harassment in your school?" Margaret continued. The administration's attempt to keep this out of the limelight would fail miserably as they were soon overwhelmed by local news media.

Chapter 23

"The Ultimate choice"

Conrad went to the hospital to meet up with his son Jordan who was there to complete his screening to be a potential bone marrow donor for his friend Harry Jr.

Conrad received word his 9am appointment cancelled which surprised him greatly. She seemed enthusiastic about the meeting. He allowed the reschedule as it gave him an opportunity to meet Jordan at Houston General hospital. When he arrived, he walked into the waiting room and texted Jordan he would be waiting for him when he completed his tests.

By chance he ran into his neighbor Harry Sr. and after exchanging awkward greetings, Harry got right to the point.

"I've decided, and my wife agrees with me that we're going to decline your family's offer. We won't allow your son to be the bone marrow transplant donor for our son Harry Sr. said to Conrad.

So, you would allow your son to die rather than accept the gift of life offered to you through us? replied Conrad. You couldn't possibly understand our decision. Said Harry Sr. "Oh I understand your decision Harry. It's based on racial hate, pride, and lies about racial superiority you and your group have been teaching. You can't make a rational decision consumed by hate! Conrad said emphatically.

You think you know something about us? Harry interjected. All you know is what you are allowed to know; our movement is above you, Mr. CEO. Said Harry with disdain.

Above me huh? I found your online pseudonym, the name

you've been hiding behind online. "Blood and Soil" right? I was planning to wait for Harry Jr. to come out of this health crisis before I acted on the information. All the hate, the nastiness against immigrants, the foolishness about Jews taking over the world you spew out online. But I can see you have been too consumed by hate to continue in your current position at HEE so your time there is over.

Your hate now affects everything you do, every decision you make, even your movements. You've become it and it has become you Conrad retorted. You have lost yourself Harry, you're now living outside of reality in an imaginary world. One where everyone who doesn't look like you is your enemy. Conrad continued.

That Quantum Engineering education works for you huh? Harry said. But you still don't have white blood. "My freedom of speech is protected by the first amendment. You can fire me, but you can't stop our movement. We've moved into all areas of life and society Harry said. "We must secure the existence of our people and a future for white children" he continued.

I also understand the phrase you just used is being hidden from everyday Americans online. In pictures, and other areas of society. 1488 right Harry? Said Conrad. That's the code you racist and people who think like you identify one another with? It's used online, in artwork, books, it's hidden from everyday Americans, but recognizable to other racist. The 14 is shorthand for the slogan you just used, those 14 words "We must secure the existence of our people and a future for white children." And the 88 is code for the 8th letter in the alphabet HH (Heil Hitler).

Secure it from who Harry, other Americans? The problem with you and your members is you believe everyone else is responsible for everything that goes wrong in your life. Every regret. Every setback.

Because of your hate, you can't find contentment; you have everything but still it's not enough and it never will be. Being a multi-millionaire is not enough for you, you can't even enjoy your own life. You have to make sure others who don't look like you suffer or lack sufficient resources Conrad said.

You're smart, but also naïve replied Harry. "Our new mission becoming mainstream; we're putting people into everyday positions. School teachers, Policemen, Judges, and Congressmen. People every day Americans can identify with. One day we'll have someone as President! A white man who can identify with the white man's struggle. How else can America achieve its greatness again accept that a true white American leads us said Harry.

I can see by the expression on your face you think people who believe what I believe are monsters. Because we speak up for our own people. I'm a great family man who wants what is best for his family Harry continued.

Family man? You're so far gone you would sacrifice your own son to this "movement" replied Conrad.

I am not sacrificing my son; God will find a better way. One which doesn't involve the tainting of pure white Christian blood said Harry.

Christian? Conrad said shaking his head and managing a laugh at the absurdity. Jesus never burned a cross, he died on one! I don't feel love coming from you. Emanating from you is something evil, something sinister.

Apparently, your group think that it's not evil because you're not wearing a hood over your heads and carrying torches? But you're worst because you have no shame for your wickedness, you in fact openly flaunt it and then refer to yourselves as white Protestant Christians despite your open rebellion against God. Hate makes people like you ok with saying anything no matter how irrational it sounds. Sadly, it also makes others believe anything. Conrad said.

I stand up for God, family, and America. We want to return America to its greatness Harry said. You believe that every advancement from another race takes away from you?

Apparently, your God has a limited supply of resources, limited opportunities. "My God doesn't run out of supply!" Conrad replied with emphasis. Conrad and Harry stared at each other for a moment; sizing up one another.

"Harry, the flaw in what you believe is you think you can control or manage your hate. Reserve it for certain people and live a "normal life". That you can manage hate's effects so it won't impact your own family, and reserve it only for those who are the object of your hate."

I was reading this book Harry titled "Who's Killing Prayer in the Church?" In it the author talks about people like you who attempt to "manage hate," believing they can live a "normal life" while hating others. He writes "I know three things for certain when it comes to hate. 1. Hate corrupts, 2. Hate consumes (takes over you and leads you where it wants to take you) 3. Hate's source is Satan. Conrad finished.

Satan huh? I'd rather have his blood than yours! Said Harry as he walked away.

Not long afterwards Harry and his wife Judy sat in the hospital waiting room hoping for some positive news in came Dr. McKenzie. She informed them that despite their best efforts to save Harry Jr. without the bone marrow transplant they were unable to. "I'm sorry, Harry Jr. has died" Dr.

McKenzie said in a somber voice. She reiterated to them the timing was critical. I wish we had more time, but every second of every minute is crucial when a person needs a bone marrow transplant to fight off the cancer, especially leukemia. Said Dr. McKenzie.

We were heartbroken to learn we hit a snag with the young man who came in for the needed test to be the donor Jordan James. The delay proved to be detrimental to the potential survival of Harry Jr. He was both young and strong and our tests indicated he was a perfect match for your son. Dr. McKenzie continued.

Not a perfect match replied Harry Sr. We were hoping the other potential donor would surface, someone more in line with our beliefs said Harry Sr. Judy Jacobs was sobbing the entire time the doctor and Harry were talking. She lost control upon hearing the delay for the "right donor" cost Harry Jr. his life.

Chapter 24

Choices come with Short-term and Long-term consequences

Dr. Ruth McKenzie was completing one of her most excruciating weeks since coming to Houston General hospital. The weekend was filled with highs and lows and it seemed the roller coaster ride was endless. She experienced being with Harry Jr. in his final moments, waiting in vain for the bone marrow transplant donor to be approved only to be setback by the family. Now Dr. McKenzie was again meeting with Andre Jackson whose daughter she did save, but his wife was murdered.

Dr. McKenzie was giving Andre an update on the status of Renae, but with another goal in mind - convincing Andre to receive the grief counseling she believed he would need to move forward with his life.

Mr. Jackson, here is the card for Dr. Louis Hernandez. He will be in later today, please call his office to schedule an appointment she said handing him the card. I'll set up the appointment with him some time in the future but first, I need to work some things out myself. Deal with some of my own personal issues Andre said.

The journey is yours, the work will be for you to complete, but that's what the doctor is for, to *help* you get through times like these replied Dr. McKenzie. I appreciate his job Andre said. However, you don't understand everything that has gotten me and my family to this point. You don't know the whole picture.

See all this truly is my fault! My wife's death, my daughter being shot and in this hospital, it's all the result of my own bad choices, my own personal decisions. I put what I knew was right to the side for personal career advancement. I told myself it was for some grand idea, a higher purpose, but at the end of the day it was for selfish ambition Andre said.

I may not see the whole picture, but I know no one deserves this to happen to them. Whatever choices you've made I'm sure at the time you thought they were for the best Dr. McKenzie said.

They sat in silence for a moment before Andre answered. "I stood face to face with my choices and I have no one to blame for them but myself. Regardless of who or how it was presented to me, I knew my choices went against all that I've been taught and believe in. The values I used to get me to this position in the first place." Andre finished as he walked off.

Chapter 25

Choices with harsh realities attached

Dr. Louis Hernandez was on his way to visit his childhood and best friend. Growing up in Houston's 5th ward, He couldn't believe 20 years had passed since the tragic incident that changed the life of three different families.

Alex Alvarez was a rising star in their neighborhood. A brilliant student who always made straight A's on his report card and was never in trouble. Also, as one of the best baseball players in the state, Alex was destined for greatness; he already was being recruited by several colleges. He easily was voted Homecoming King their senior year as well as "most likely to succeed".

Dr. Hernandez shook his head in disbelief. Blown way that Alex has been in prison for the last 20 years, serving a life sentence in the Texas state penitentiary for a double murder.

As he was making the long walk through the prison corridors to the inmate visitation area his mind replayed the day over in his head just as in previous times. A day now imprinted in his memory despite his best efforts to have it removed. Somehow it still lingered like a bad odor you couldn't get out of a room.

Alex bought a gun on a whim one day as he and Louis were walking home from school. They were approached by someone in the neighborhood who was selling a stolen handgun. The sight of the gun piqued the interest of Alex. What are you doing man you don't need a gun? Louis decried. All it's going to do is cause trouble he said.

Relax man, Alex said. I'm not going to hurt anyone, it's just for fun. I just want to be able to hold one, maybe do some practice shooting. Don't be such a coward Alex laughed attempting to make light of it. Alex if you ever get caught with a gun in school you'll be kicked out said Louis.

I'm not going to take the gun to school man; in fact, I'm not going to carry it around I just want to hold it and keep it at home Alex said.

They were on the basketball court enjoying a friendly game when out of nowhere a fight broke out between Alex and another kid. As calm was being restored, two others emerged from the sideline attempting to confront him. Alex was now packing his belongings into his gym bag. The two boys started to head towards Alex when he abruptly pulled the gun from the bag. As Louis yelled out "Alex no!" He fired three shots hitting two people killing them. One an innocent bystander 300 feet away who was the brother of Dr. Ruth McKenzie; his current colleague and confidant at Houston General hospital.

Wow! Life is so uncertain these days; one bad choice and man said Louis. The doors to the prison swung open and in walked Alex escorted by a prison guard and shackled by his hands and feet. An astounding sight no one could have ever imagined. The least likely person from the neighborhood brought in as a life-long criminal.

The two childhood friends, now adults had come from the same roots and community but it produced vastly different results.

Dr. Hernandez was now a PH. D and grief counselor at Houston General as well a lecturer at the University of Houston. Alex Alvarez was serving a life sentence for a double murder.

They talked for about 15 minutes the way they normally did over these past 20 years. Neither one ever bringing up the tragic incident which led to Alex's current circumstance.

Usually they talked about family, sports, even religion, always avoiding the "elephant in the room". This time Louis was determined to finally address the past so they could move forward.

I've been coming to see you for the past 20 years Alex and we've never once talked about that day in the park. How you ended up here said Louis. I know it's like a ghost in the room with us when we meet, but I haven't been able to bring myself to talk about it with you. I guess now is as good a time as any. Alex replied.

Twenty years later I still can't believe you opened fire and killed those people said Louis.

I did not wake up intending to hurt or shoot anyone. It's the worst moment of my life, one I wish I could take back. It's a decision that haunts me in my mind every day said Alex.

I remember it like it was yesterday, the words of the judge at my sentencing. I had just finished apologizing to the families of the victim and to the court Alex continued and then quoting the judge who said.

"This courtroom is frequently a place of regret, a place where apologies are often given by people with no prior compassion or thought for others. Although I'm sure young man you wish you could go back in time and make a better choice on that day. However, that is not our reality. I've been going over your record prior to sentencing and it saddens me to see your history. The talent you've wasted. This is your first offence. You were a straight A student and I've been told you were destined to do great things. Unfortunately,

choices have results, actions have consequences, and the law requires justice."

Those were the judge's words and I guess I must agree with him. Alex said.

I have learned that choices have consequences both short term and long term. Remember I always told you how one day I wanted to become a doctor Alex continued.

You were the smartest kid in school. The smartest I have ever met including my six years of college. Louis replied.

It doesn't matter how smart you are in school if you make bad choices in life. A lot of us waste the gifts God has given to us, especially when we're young.

There are smart young guys brought into this prison every day. It's like the story of the prodigal son in the bible. I always thought it was about other things, but the word prodigal means wasteful.

The atmosphere in the room was starting to grow intense, heavy as their conversation permeated the room.

They hadn't realized it, but they were now the center of attention in the meeting room for inmates and their families. Five or six other inmates were receiving family visits at the same time all now drawn into the conversation of Alex and Louis. Captivated by its passion, its lessons, and listening intently.

It was so stupid of you, buying the gun that day we were walking home from school. I have to admit I'm still upset at you for buying it. Your choice changed both of our lives forever! Said Louis in anger, growing emotional.

Alex replied, I wish I had not started down this path. Some roads are easier to get off than others. I didn't choose death over life the moment I shot those people. It was a choice I made a long time before that. I just didn't think I would end up here said Alex loudly. Speaking as if he wanted everyone in the room to hear him.

The visitation time was now winding down; the time seemingly stood still for them as they were engrossed in a long overdue conversation. Dr. Louis Hernandez stood up as the prison guard motioned to him to start moving. He was now full of emotion, crying as his friend was speaking, reflecting on their friendship; what might have been.

Remembering they had already left the house to go to the playground on that day when Alex went back inside to retrieve something. As he was leaving, he turned with tears in his eyes one last time to look back at Alex. Why'd you have to go back inside to get the gun Alex? Louis said half talking and half sobbing from the passion of the moment. Struggling to get the question out.

I didn't go back inside to get the gun; I went back inside to get my hat. The gun just happened to be lying there. Said Alex.

Chapter 26

When the choice of hate is stronger than love

It was now three days since the death of Harry Jacobs Jr. along with the prevention of a mass shooting on the same day at the Sun Park High School.

Judy Jacobs was at home sitting alone on the couch in a daze starring into the distance, eyes wide open but seeing nothing. Contemplating the life of her son, attempting to remember the good times they shared.

In a tumultuous, world-wind of a week he was now gone much too soon. Dying from the effects of Leukemia. A dangerous bone cancer after not receiving a desperately needed bone marrow transplant in time.

The words of Dr. McKenzie along with her husband's response replayed in her mind continuously over the past three days. "We were heartbroken to learn we hit a snag with the young man who came in for the needed test to be the donor Jordan James. The delay proved to be detrimental to the potential survival of Harry Jr. He was both young and strong and our tests indicated he was a perfect match for your son." Dr. McKenzie continued.

Not a perfect match replied Harry Sr. "We were hoping the other potential donor would surface someone more in line with our beliefs."

Like an old broken record or a faucet that wouldn't stop leaking the repetition of the scene became distressing, agonizing, and torturous. A bad song she couldn't get out of her head despite her best efforts even screaming at herself to stop it did nothing.

Both she and Harry Sr. had isolated themselves to certain areas of the house; both alone despite the presence of one another.

On the third day Harry Sr. finally emerged from the basement of his home to check on his wife.

Harry had been unable to eat a thing in the three days, instead spending the entire time waddling in despair. His tears were the food that sustained him. The extreme bouts of disappointment he would succumb to ever since he was a child was now back. Only this time multiplied due to prior choices to not seek help; it felt like a weight magnified over time.

They both sat in silence for a few minutes before Judy finally spoke up.

"I've already filed for a divorce Harry. I filed a day after we came back from the hospital while you were hiding in your cave" she said.

Harry simply sat there in silence not showing any reaction. The normally submissive Judy Jacobs then kept going. "You've been working hard your whole life attempting to please your father, HEE Inc., Rex and his white supremacist groupies and no matter what you've accomplished, you have not been able to find contentment. It's like you're in a prison and that's because you are. You should have been seeking God's approval not men" Judy said.

Harry looked up at his wife and tearfully responded. "God did not answer my prayers and save my son."

God answered our prayers, you just didn't like the answer she swiftly intervened. You chose Rex and his hate groupies over God and his love; racial ideology over the life of our son. You simply chose to allow our son to die! Yelled Judy.

"I have to take some of the responsibility for my complicity in the face of your hatred she admitted. I was actively participating with my silence. But I have learned that anytime we sit quietly in the presence of hatred, we are just as guilty as the person who is spewing hate, maybe worse!" she said.

I was strategically placed in a position of influence by God and I chose to do nothing.

I'll be leaving the house in about an hour catching the train out of town for a few days, but I won't be returning to this house. You can have it. I wouldn't want to live here anymore without our son. You should be hearing from my attorney soon. Goodbye Harry. I hope you get the help you need to get through this. Judy Jacobs then left the house hoping never to see Harry again.

Chapter 27

Blinded by our choices

    A few days later Harry Jacobs, a man with a crushed spirit, finally got up the strength to leave the house.

He decided he needed the company of his "brothers", the other members of his Nazi group. Harry drove to the home of the group's leader and the man who recruited him to the group - Rex. Unknown to Harry, Rex was the second person who was a potential match for his son's bone marrow transplant. He kept the information hidden fearing it would somehow show him as having the same blood as James Jordan a young black man.

    Upon entering the home of Rex, they exchanged greetings. Sorry for your loss brother said Rex. I was sure God would step in and provide an answer for you and your son. "God works in mysterious ways sometimes" Rex said pretending to have empathy for Harry.

Thanks, brother. said Harry. The second potential donor never made himself known; never came forward for testing.

I'm glad you allowed me to come by today, I needed someone to talk to. I knew you would be there for me in my time of grieving even if no one else would said Harry.

Of course, Replied Rex feigning excitement. Us pure white men must stick together especially in times like these.

    You know with all these immigrants, niggers, and Jews coming into our country we must stick together said Rex. At least I can say I preserved our bloodline Harry replied. I stuck to our teachings and didn't allow the pure white blood to be tainted with that nigger blood! Harry continued. Perking up a bit for the first time since his son's death. He started to get his old look back in his eyes as he and Rex went back and forth with their racist doctrine for about a half hour.

Harry then shifted gears. Conrad James found me online and has been investigating some of the activities of our movement. I think he wants to expose us Harry said. How did he find that information? Rex asked. They say he's a genius, able to think on another plane. Three dimensionally or something off the wall Harry answered.

A genius? Thee dimensionally? Rex said in amazement. We're going to have to get rid of him. His day is coming. We'll make him wish he never left Chicago to come here. We can't allow information like that to get out about some nigger! I agree replied Harry.

I have some good news for you Harry, to lift you in your time of grieving. "Because you've done such a great job with our online content and recruitment, I have been instructed by our National Office to offer you our newly created position of Homeland Internal Defense if you are interested. Rex offered.

What would that include? Harry asked.

We need someone who can monitor political or social protests and unrest in the United States. Potential hot spots where protest may be brewing for disruptive change to our way of life. You would head up our crisis response to those areas. Be ready to deploy our membership throughout the country at a moment's notice. A quick response, agile team that can move in quickly and infiltrate their protests and confound those who would force change on this great nation, on our way of life! Said Rex.

These immigrants have been attempting to change our

world with their protests for years and we have been working behind the scenes manipulating them, distracting from the real issues they complain about. That will be your primary responsibility to distract! mislead! agitate!

We want you to organize teams and formulate plans of action to create havoc during times of protest. You will be in charge of turning their protests into mayhem, looting, and violent confrontations. Be subversive! We already have people positioned in the news media that you can coordinate your efforts with so that the focus will be more on the destruction of property, looting, and violence and away from the real issues that threaten our way of life.

Lastly we want you to help us to coordinate the continued flow of guns into the country and especially the inner cities. We have people in positions to prevent any gun legislation from happening so that the violence and mass incarceration can continue and they can kill one another while we profit off it. "1488" forever!

Harry smiled with satisfaction. This guy Conrad James could be a dangerous threat to our movement. Harry said to Rex.

So were those niggers Huey Newton, Malcom X, Medgar Evers, and Martin Luther King, and looked what we did to them.

Why do you think they're still out there marching and chanting after all these years Rex replied emphatically?

We know how to get into the middle of their protests and cause mayhem and anarchy, create fear of change amongst the American public. We have people with expertise in the psychology of crowd behavior, how to blend into one, incite them into violence and move out.

Then we allow the natural instincts of a mob mentality to take over like we did in the days of lynching - those were the good ole days. We did that to white folks so how much easier it is going to be to do it to those people.

I'll leave you and your wife to your evening Harry said as he got up to leave. Thanks for taking the time to chat with me he said. Anytime my brother! Replied Rex.

After Harry left Rexnord Rutherford sat there with a drink in his hand thinking how much he could use Harry to carry out his anti-immigration agenda. "Every US President needs and anti-immigration person in his cabinet." Rex said to himself. His wife who was sitting in the next room listening to them entered breaking the quietness. Why didn't you tell him you were the other donor she asked?

I told you before, I can't have people thinking the blood of a nigger and mine are the same or can serve the same purpose!

But you may have been able to save his son's life. She replied. You're still missing the higher purpose of our movement Rex said. I'm sorry about his son, but our movement like any war requires sacrifices, collateral damages.

War? She asked.

Yes, war! Rex said. We're in a war to take back our country. We can no longer allow all of these immigrants, niggers, and especially Jews to take over this once great country. I'm planning on running for President of the United States one day and something like this blood match could hurt my chances and the movement.

You actually think people will vote for you with all of your hateful rhetoric? Your demeaning and nasty tone towards others? Talking down to women and calling them names? His wife asked.

You'd be surprised who and what people are willing to vote for. I know how to tap into their fears, exploit their inner emotions and natural biases, give them a false hope. Only a pure white man can lead this country back to its prior greatness replied Rex.

Chapter 28

Choose Life defined

It was the end of a week that would never be forgotten in the Houston suburb of Sun Park, TX. The high school won its first football state championship. While in the midst of the celebrations the star quarterback was diagnosed with Leukemia. As the town was rallying around him and encouraging people to register as potential donors at bethematch.com Harry Jr. died.

Now the local news media was again swarming the Sun Park High School campus. The news was breaking of a potential mass shooting there that had been narrowly averted.

Margaret Jones, the mother of a student being mercilessly bullied by other students received a last-second phone call from Harry Jr. while on her way to a meeting she described as an opportunity of a lifetime. She made the choice to act immediately on the news, cancelling the meeting and instead speeding to the high school. Her decision likely saved the life of many students including her son Oliver Jones and his best friend Henry Allen the two potential shooters.

Margaret Jones later in the day went to the hospital to thank Harry Jr. for standing up to help her son only to find out Harry Jr. had died. The heartbreaking news compelled her to immediately go see Judy Jacobs, Harry's mother.

Margaret shared an emotional testimony with her of how Harry helped to save the life of her son and the lives of several other students in his final moments. They sat down and hugged each other for about an hour cherishing the heroic deed of Harry Jr. Added to all this Daphne Jackson, the wife of the news executive of the year Andre Jackson was murdered in her home.

The mayor, other local political, religious, and business leaders called for a summit to address these issues and their impact on Sun Park. They decided they wanted to hold a town hall meeting at the Sun Park High School. The entire community would be invited to come out to address any concerns.

The meeting was being promoted as an opportunity for community healing, community building, and unity. It was decided the Keynote speaker at the forum would be the newcomer to the community who had attracted so much new excitement and energy Conrad James.

Never one to sit idly by while there were issues to be addressed, Conrad James had already taken steps to bring the town together. When he heard about the choice Margaret Jones made putting aside personal and career advancement to save the life of her son and others, Conrad immediately reached out to her to reschedule their appointment.

He in fact already hired her to be the newly created community liaison for HEE Inc. stating "this is an example of the type of person we want working for us."

Conrad also was personally leading a team now working on initiatives to be announced at the town-hall meeting.

The day started with small group sessions of no more than 20 people per group with a designated team leader. Meetings defined by their remorse, sorrow, shame.

Parents and students bonded for the shared purpose of community unity.

The town hall became therapeutic, catharsis for a community badly in need of healing. An opportunity to release the pent-up emotions brought to the surface by the roller coaster week with the near mass shooting at the school becoming a flashpoint for change.

But now the excitement was building, and anticipation saturated the air. The town gathered inside of the large school auditorium for the day's ending presentation by Conrad James.

Conrad confidently stepped to the podium.

"Choose Life!" He said pausing for effect. That statement sounds simple enough and it also sounds logical, or like common sense for no one would intentionally choose death, would they?

Our first reaction to someone choosing death would probably be to think of someone struggling with a mental illness, depression, or in a state of despair that has overwhelmed them. Making them feel they could no longer carry the burden of life.

To choose life is even encouraged by God himself in scripture. Deuteronomy 30:19 says, "I have set before you life and death, blessing and cursing: therefore, "**choose life.**"

What this scripture is giving us is a principle for life. A guiding principle we can turn to and live our life by. It's not referring to a singular event, a specific choice, or even a moment in time.

The scripture doesn't have to address every specific issue or circumstance you will encounter because it is an overarching theme that guides your life.

You don't have to go around repeating it in your head or

have it tattooed on your arm. It suggests a choice of lifestyle and way of living.

To "choose life" is shaped in your quiet moments and personal time alone. It's a decision to allow this principle to guide your life and therefore your decisions.

Long before we are involved in any type of interaction, dispute, or even confrontation with someone, we have already made decisions and choices that have shaped our responses to the situation.

Choices don't happen in the heat of the moment, reactions do.

A kid who is in prison for life due to gun violence started down a path initiated by the bad choices of the past either from them or their parents long before his act of violence. We must learn to have a process for decision making.

What I do is live as a man of faith. I start my day off in prayer and I meditate on my morning devotional time throughout the day. If that's not who you are you still need some type of process to help shape and mold your choices throughout the day.

Whether its contemplating some of your mothers and grandmothers "old sayings", getting favorite quotes from people in history, or people you respect and look up to.

The bottom line is you can't wait until you're faced with the choice of violence or walking away, lying or being truthful, stealing or giving. Don't simply rely upon spur of the moment and split-second decision making. You need a process for decision making. The process becomes your filter which alerts you when something is outside of the boundaries of the person you have decided to be.

This filter then can reject following the crowd to do

destructive things, bad advice/suggestions from others, and even your own inner bad thoughts. To "choose life" is that process.

A guiding principle to direct your path. Leading you down the correct path in life and providing direction to a better way of living.

When faced with the proverbial "fork in the road" to "choose life" is the light that shines on the correct path to take and allow you to make great life choices, filtering out erroneous information even if it's coming from a friend or loved one. Empowering you to reject it as something you do not aspire to become.

Are you going to be a person known for love or hate, integrity or dishonesty, violence or understanding?

Do you have the needed strength to step away from the computer or must you always press send no matter how out of bounds your comments were? You don't have to become a bully on social media regardless of what the crowd is doing. A lot of people are on social media displaying a lack of discipline and unfiltered thoughts.

Conrad James now had the crowd made up of both students and parents on the edge of their seats. Some were emotional others listening so intently they were unable to take their focus off the charismatic newcomer to their town. Those who started out looking at their phones or other devices set them aside as Conrad commanded the room. He laid out his thoughts with precision, yet empathy for others derived from a sincere heart, looking to heal a broken and hurting community. He then moved on to laying out some of the initiatives he and his team wanted to present.

Conrad paused for a moment allowing the crowd to take in

the message he was presenting.

Scanning the large crowd there was an air of expectation as Conrad took a moment of reflection in front of the thousands of people peering at him.

Harry Jacobs Jr. had accomplished a lot in his short life Conrad said. But he also showed how one person with both an open mind, and heart can overcome any obstacle and make a lasting impact on his community.

With his last breath of life, he took a stand against bullying and against hatred making his final phone call to Margaret Jones with his last ounce of strength. Harry saved the life of several people who are here in this room with us today Conrad said. Bringing gasps of shock from the crowd.

Displaying the heart of the type of person he became, Harry didn't do what a lot of us have become guilty of in America - allowing some of the great creeds that we say we hold dearly as Americans to become empty or meaningless. Instead, he lived them out by his actions. Words like

"One Nation, Under God," "Indivisible with liberty and justice for all".

"We hold these truths to be self-evident that all men are created equal."

Words that for far too many have become hollow, stated robotically while our actions work against the very spirit of those words.

To them they have become slogans, almost having the tone of a marketing jingle! Conrad stated emphatically.

Chapter 29

Choose Life lived

I would now like to lay out some of the initiatives my team and I have been working on. We believe problems have solutions and that we have a moral obligation as a community to explore them. However, ultimately no change can substitute for the changing of the heart.

First. We've already designed computer programs and algorithms to be used to counteract online bullying, victimization, and hate groups. The program is set up to identify, monitor, and expose hate group activity including illegal firearms purchases and drugs.

Secondly, the development of a website to track and display who they are and what they are doing. This website will be used for the dispensing of information on the activities of these evil groups. The purveyors of hate, bullies, and illegal gun buyers and sellers. Even though being evil is a choice, we will not sit in silence and allow it to flourish in our community, in our country.

We'll focus on their political activities and financial contributions to political campaigns. Prominently displaying what politicians accept contributions from them, and the extent of their involvement in these groups. But we won't stop at politics.

Anyone involved in the legal system, judges, lawyers, policemen will also be brought out into the open on this website.

Hate groups, bully's, and violence advocates like to point to the First Amendment of the Constitution (Freedom of

Speech) to justify their right to say any hateful or hurtful thing. Well we also have that right. A right to expose them for who they are.

You're no longer going to be allowed to be a judge, school teacher, policemen, or even a politician and participate in those types of activities in secret. We have resolved to shine a light on your dark activities. If people still want to nominate, elect for political office, or advance those types of people then it'll simply reveal the true heart of America.

Lastly. We have collaborated with the Mayor to declare the day of his death and his saving of life Harry Jacobs Jr day in the town of Sun Park, TX. A "take your stand against bullying day!" This day will have as its focus to stand-up against mistreatment in all forms. There will be a large campaign encouraging youths and others to stand-up, and speak up, against intimidation at school and online.

We know that kids who are being bullied at school miss up to two days a week because of the tormenting. Also, that suicide is the second leading cause of death for young people. We believe these measures will help to counteract those numbers by bringing awareness and weeding out this problem.

Additionally, during this week we will be presenting a deserving student or youth with the Harry Jacobs Jr. "take your stand against bullying award." Also, we will be partnering with bethematch.com to lead a bone marrow drive in honor of Harry Jacobs Jr. Who died while waiting for a potential donor to come forward. We hope these measures will capture the true spirt of who we are as a people.

Conrad James paused for a moment. Observing the emotions of the crowd, he allowed them the opportunity to take in his message and digest some of the proposed initiatives he wanted to implement. Shifting gears, he wanted to end the presentation with personal accountability as his main theme. The primary instrument of change for any community he believed was personal accountability.

It's not just talent alone that allows some to "make it" and others not to. A big part of the process is their life choices, lifestyle, and a lack of discipline. These variables prevent some from fulfilling the promise of being who they were intended to be.

Our choices set in motion consequences we will live through at some point in the future.

Choices and consequences have a cause and effect relationship. Choices lead us down roads usually we won't see until we get there. Some bad choices will make you go further than you planned to go, stay longer than you planned to stay, and cost you more than you planned to pay.

Conrad continued all of us at some point in our lives will come face to face with decisions which will test our level of personal character and integrity. A choice we can't blame on anyone else. Our fork in the road that could determine our direction in life for years to come. It's instant gratification and short-term thinking that hurts people the most in these situations.

I'm reminded of how my mom used to handle those situations when we were faced with hard times.

We were living well below the government declared "poverty line" on Chicago's Westside. In fact, we would have to save and build to get to the "poverty line". It would have been a step up for us. My mom would be faced with a dilemma at times of doing something she knew was wrong but would provide us with a much-needed instant relief from our harsh circumstances.

She'd always pause for a moment, then look at me, sometimes with tears in her eyes and she'd paraphrase a scripture from the book of Proverbs. (She would always misquote it, but in her life, she nailed it). I'll give it to you now to be used as a lamp on dark roads to "choosing life". *Proverbs 22:1 "A good name is more desirable than great riches; to be esteemed is better than silver and gold."* Despite our financial hardship, she was determined to hold on to her personal integrity and teach me to do the same. Refusing to lie, cheat, steal, or compromise herself for personal gain.

My mom didn't graduate from college or anything, but I later came to understand she developed a process for her decision making. She never called it that, but I later would define it by the acronym PCEE. She would **P**ause, **C**ontemplate, **E**valuate, **E**levate above her circumstances.

To conclude, protect your name. Compromising your personal integrity is compromising your name for short-term gratification. It takes years maybe even a lifetime to build a good name or reputation, but it can be torn down in an instant by one poor decision, or one bad choice.

Conrad then slowing walked off the stage leaving to a thundering ovation of cries mixed with cheers.

Harry Sr, Paul Wilson, and Rex the leaders of their hate group sat quietly in a corner of the packed auditorium lurking in the background. Their moods a stark contradiction from the emotion of the rest of the crowd. The hatred they were teaching and spreading now consumed them, rendering them unteachable.

The occasion was described as a community healing

session, a time for unity, however they came with a different motivation - to plot against Conrad and plan their next move. All they could do as Conrad was being honored by the crowd was to burn with an intense hatred and anger even amid love and healing. "We're going to have to do something about him" they agreed with one another.

Conrad and Janice James stood in the back corridor of the packed auditorium listening to the sounds from the crowd. Some were still cheering, some crying, while others expressing joy through laughter. They were thinking about the path their lives had taken bringing them from Chicago to Houston. Conrad couldn't help but think of his mother Sabrina James and the early days of their life in Henry Horner projects. Conrad was now a leader in his community. It was an unlikely result, but against all odds he "made it" out.

"You are a superhero!" Janice said to Conrad as they took in the moment both listening to the emotions of the people milling around. "Superhero? I'm just a man, I don't possess any superpowers." Conrad laughed in response. Sure, you do Janice said. Your Spirit is Holy, and some of your superpowers are empathy and compassion for others, a heart for justice, and the ability to embrace hateful people. To forgive and love far beyond the limits of any "normal person" Janice added.

Conrad looked at Janice and said "my momma loved the people of Henry Horner projects. I learned a lot from them to, they taught me how to survive and overcome obstacles, if it wasn't for the people there, I wouldn't be in this position right now.

My momma just wanted to show me that coming from Henry Horner projects you could still dream. She taught me to believe in a future she herself would never see. A promise by America yet to be kept, and hope deferred for far too long. That you could still accomplish the desires of your heart, but someone needed to show you the vision. If you could see it, you can do it. You simply have to "choose life".

www.ingramcontent.com/pod-product-compliance
Lightning Source LLC
LaVergne TN
LVHW011839060526
838200LV00054B/4106